Sizing Up the Enemy . . .

The smaller of the pair took a few steps forward and stopped short before putting himself within Slocum's reach. That made Slocum's decision clear as to who should be on the receiving end of his next swing. The larger bushwhacker was about his size, and Slocum met him with a punch that came all the way around in an arc and ended at the side of the man's head. Ironically, Slocum's knuckles hit the spot that their other partner should have found with the butt of his gun. Striking just behind and slightly above the other man's ear, Slocum's fist landed hard enough to put that fellow onto his knees. Once there, Slocum finished him off with another blow that didn't require as much finesse. His knee swung forward to pound into the kneeling man's face and send him sprawling onto his back.

"What are you waiting fer?" the smaller attacker shouted to the larger one. "Shoot!"

Slocum may have been drunk. He may have been wobbly after taking that first crack to his head. He may have even been tuckered out after spending the last day and a half playing cards in the Sunset Saloon. But none of those things was enough to make him forget about the Remington revolver holstered at his side. His hand drifted toward the pistol, lingering a scant inch above it as he locked eyes with the bigger man and said, "Yeah. Go ahead. Shoot."

JAKE LOGAN

SLOCUM AND THE REDHEADED DEVIL

J

JOVE BOOKS, NEW YORK

THE BERKLEY PUBLISHING GROUP
Published by the Penguin Group
Penguin Group (USA) LLC
375 Hudson Street, New York, New York 10014

USA • Canada • UK • Ireland • Australia • New Zealand • India • South Africa • China

penguin.com

A Penguin Random House Company

SLOCUM AND THE REDHEADED DEVIL

A Jove Book / published by arrangement with the author

For information, address: The Berkley Publishing Group,
a division of Penguin Group (USA) LLC,
375 Hudson Street, New York, New York 10014.

ISBN: 978-0-515-15481-8

PUBLISHING HISTORY
Jove mass-market edition / July 2014

PRINTED IN THE UNITED STATES OF AMERICA

10 9 8 7 6 5 4 3 2 1

Cover illustration by Sergio Giovine.

1

Slocum had been in Pico Alto, Nevada, for just under two weeks before he was knocked in the back of the head by the butt of a pistol. Cracking a man's skull wasn't as straightforward as it might seem. At least, it wasn't if the person doing the cracking meant to put their target down in one blow. Any fool with an arm and a Colt could give someone a splitting headache. It took a bit of know-how to make that one shot count for something. When Slocum was on the receiving end of a shot like that, one was all he was going to allow.

Having just left the Sunset Saloon, Slocum had been rounding the corner of First and Hyde streets. He'd had more than his share of whiskey, and his eyes stung from the haze of too many cheap cigars being smoked in that place. Although he would have liked to have a few more excuses for why the bushwhackers were able to get so close to him, Slocum knew the whiskey was the main culprit. By the time he heard heavy footsteps coming up behind him, all he could do was turn halfway around as the butt of that pistol was introduced to his head.

An inch or two in any direction and the blow would have landed true. Instead, Slocum was knocked somewhere on top of his head toward the back. It rang his bell for certain, but didn't affect his vision any worse than all the liquor he'd poured down his throat earlier that night. When he wheeled around to face his attackers, Slocum was unsteady on his feet, but the fire that swelled up in him went a long way in making up for it.

There were three of them. Two wore bandannas that partially covered their faces, and the third was caked in so much dirt that he might as well have been masked. The closest man was the biggest and outweighed Slocum by a good margin. Although he was armed, he'd been the one to take the first swing, which meant he was still holding his pistol by the barrel when Slocum came at him. Despite the anger behind Slocum's punch, his balance was still impeded by the knock he'd taken. Of course, the whiskey still didn't help much.

"Take this, you son of a b—" was all the big man got out before Slocum's fist caught him in the mouth. As he reeled back from the punch, the big man's two partners rushed in to try and put Slocum down.

The smaller of the pair took a few steps forward and stopped short before putting himself within Slocum's reach. That made Slocum's decision clear as to who should be on the receiving end of his next swing. The larger bushwhacker was about his size, and Slocum met him with a punch that came all the way around in an arc and ended at the side of the man's head. Ironically, Slocum's knuckles hit the spot that their other partner should have found with the butt of his gun. Striking just behind and slightly above the other man's ear, Slocum's fist landed hard enough to bring that fellow to his knees. Once there, Slocum finished him off with another blow that didn't require as much finesse. His knee swung forward to pound into the kneeling man's face and send him sprawling onto his back.

"What are you waiting fer?" the smaller attacker shouted to the larger one. "Shoot!"

Slocum may have been drunk. He may have been wobbly after taking that first crack to his head. He may have even been tuckered out after spending the last day and a half playing cards in the Sunset Saloon. But none of those things was enough to make him forget about the Remington revolver holstered at his side. His hand drifted toward the pistol, lingering a scant inch above it as he locked eyes with the bigger man and said, "Yeah. Go ahead. Shoot."

"Shit, Cal," the big man grunted. "This vagrant ain't got nothin' worth stealin' anyhow."

The smaller man's voice was a coarse hiss as he whispered, "Too late to worry about that. We started this. We gotta see it through."

Actually, the big man was speaking the God's honest truth. Apart from a dollar and a quarter in his pocket, the only things Slocum carried were an old watch he'd won in the previous night's game, the key to his hotel room, and the gun on his hip. Even so, he wasn't about to roll over for the likes of these three. "Tell you what," Slocum said. "You two collect your friend down there, move along, and we can go our separate ways."

"You . . . you'll tell the law 'bout us," the big man grunted.

"What for?" Slocum asked with a shrug. "That asshole was going to hurt me," he said while tapping the downed man with his boot, "so I hurt him. You got the drop on me, but I shouldn't have let you get so close. Lesson learned."

"So . . . that's it?"

"No. You take any more time thinking over this gener-
ous offer and I'll pay back the first knock you gave me
with a few more of my own."

"Ummm . . . yeah . . . well . . ."

The larger man's eyes darted back and forth between
Slocum and something else. Something just over Slocum's
shoulder. Slocum had lost sight of the third man, but he
wasn't about to take his eyes off the big fellow with the
gun, so he took a step back to put the smaller man back
into his field of vision. When his boot was halfway to
where he wanted it to go, it bumped against something
solid. Slocum cussed under his breath, raised his left arm,
and snapped his elbow straight back.

Since the smaller man had been quiet enough to get
right behind Slocum, it wasn't much of a surprise that he
was also quick enough to avoid being hit by the elbow that
Slocum swung in his direction. The man skittered away
like the rodent he was, all but disappearing into one of the
thick shadows encroaching on either side of the narrow
street. It was well past midnight, which meant there was
more than enough darkness to use for cover. Any little
noise that was made, however, echoed like an empty tea
kettle being dropped onto a wooden floor. Slocum followed
the sound of the smaller man's steps scraping against the
dirt until he heard the louder crunch of much bigger boots
stomping after him.

Slocum took one last look and caught sight of the
smaller man darting across the street toward an alley. As
he turned back around to face the larger man, Slocum drew
the Remington in a swift motion that was barely affected
by all the whiskey flowing through his veins. Although he
cleared leather, he didn't bring the pistol's barrel up more
than an inch or so before his arm was stopped by a beefy
fist that took hold of him in an iron grip. Slocum continued

to turn and brought his left hand around to pound the big man's face. It was a glancing punch that didn't do much more than rip the bandanna away to reveal an ugly grin.

Before he knew what was happening, Slocum was wrapped up in a one-armed bear hug. The big man kept hold of Slocum's wrist while enveloping him in a mass of muscle. Once he had a hold on him, the big man lifted Slocum off his feet. Rather than waiting to be slammed down onto his ribs, neck, or back, Slocum lashed out with both legs to slam his boots into the big man's shins. It wasn't enough to force his hulking opponent to drop him, but the next bunch of flailing kicks sure did the trick.

As soon as Slocum was on his own two feet again, he backed away from the big man. The other fellow was still growling like a wounded grizzly bear, but he hadn't let go of Slocum's arm. When Slocum got a few steps away from him, the big man yanked him back as if they were a pair of clumsy ballroom dancers. Slocum felt the lack of sleep and abundance of whiskey rush in on him as he was pulled toward the big man. The world teetered around him until the only thing keeping him up was the other man's solid hold on his wrist. It took a moment for Slocum's head to stop spinning, and when it did, he was treated to the sight of the big man's face rushing straight at him.

The head butt landed solidly, thumping against a spot just above the bridge of Slocum's nose. Dark blobs formed in his eyes, and he staggered uneasily while the big man started to laugh.

"What now, little man?" Slocum's attacker grunted.

When Slocum tried twisting his hand within the other man's grasp to point his pistol at a real target, the grip around his wrist tightened until Slocum swore he felt bones grinding together. Before he was snapped like a dry twig, Slocum opened his hand to let the Remington fall from it.

The pistol dropped for less than a second before it was caught by Slocum's other hand. Even as he wrapped his fingers around the pistol's grip, Slocum could feel the other man pulling him in again for another head butt or something even worse. Either way, Slocum knew he wouldn't be able to put up much of a fight after taking whatever it was the big man intended on dishing out.

Rather than taking any sort of aim, Slocum only took enough time to make sure his gun's barrel was pointed away from him before pulling his trigger. The Remington's single blast rolled through the air, spitting a plume of black gritty smoke while driving a piece of hot lead straight down into the big man's foot. While the attacker's eyes were smug in victory only a moment ago, they were now wide in surprise and pain.

It didn't take much for Slocum to pull away from the big man after drilling a hole through his boot. The first thing he did once he was free was to take a look around to make sure nobody was going to sneak up on him again. The first man to be dropped was just now pulling himself up, so Slocum put him down again with a solid uppercut to the jaw.

The smallest bushwhacker was nowhere to be found, and the largest one was still managing to stay upright. Slocum walked up to him to place the barrel of his pistol against the giant's chest.

For a moment, Slocum seriously considered pulling his trigger even if it was just to send a message to the other two. Then Slocum took a moment to push through the whiskey haze still roiling in his skull and decided on another course of action. Lowering the pistol, he swept his leg straight across to tap his boot against the other man's freshly wounded foot. That was more than enough to topple the big man like an oak that had been set upon by a swarm of lumberjacks.

Even after the scuffle, the gunshot, and the impact of the big man's back against the ground, nobody was coming around for a look at what was going on. Slocum had only been in Pico Alto for a short time and had yet to catch more than a fleeting glimpse of the town's single lawman. The fellow was supposed to be healthy enough and a bit younger than Slocum, but spent most of his time away on business matters. Slocum didn't know if that meant riding in a posse or sitting at a creek with a fishing pole in his hand and didn't much care. For the moment, the only reason Slocum thought about the town's law at all was to make certain it wasn't charging up to give him any grief for firing his weapon in a public place. Even in a case of self-defense, a man had to answer for shooting someone. That didn't seem to be a problem, however, since the streets were just as still now as they had been when Slocum first stepped out of the Sunset Saloon.

Once his ears stopped ringing after getting knocked around, Slocum realized the street wasn't totally quiet after all. Somewhere nearby, light panting breaths could be heard. After a few more seconds, Slocum thought he heard a woman crying.

He walked forward, keeping his gun in hand but lowered at his side. The sound came from across the street. When he narrowed the source down to the alley where the third bushwhacker had escaped, he quickened his steps and brought his gun back up.

"Someone there?" he asked cautiously.

The sobbing was quickly choked off and a slender figure emerged from the alley. She was a woman in a thin, filmy dress that looked like it could have been a slip. When she stepped out of the shadows and into the pale glow of the stars, the simple flower pattern on her dress could more clearly be seen.

"Are you all right, miss?" Slocum asked.

"I am," she replied in a voice that was stronger than he'd been expecting. She batted her eyelids, looked down the alley and sharply back at Slocum. "What about you? Are you hurt?"

Slocum gingerly touched the part of his face that had been knocked the worst and felt blood on his fingers. "I been better, but I also been a whole lot worse. Were you knocked aside when that fella took off down the alley?"

As she got closer to him, it became clear that the woman hadn't been crying after all. Her cheeks were smeared with some dust that had been kicked up and glistened from sweat, but none of that was much of a surprise considering the ruckus that had taken place around her or the heat of the summer night in which it had happened. The expression on her face showed anything but fear, however. In fact, she looked excited with just a touch of nervousness thrown in. "He did shove me," she said anxiously. "But no harm was done. He seemed to be in a real big hurry. Is he a friend of yours?"

"Not hardly. Do you know where he got to?"

Pointing down the alley, she replied, "That way." Shrugging, she added, "That's all I saw. Sorry."

"All right then."

"I should go."

"Just give those two over there a wide berth," Slocum said as she started walking down the alley.

She looked toward the two men in the street, but wasn't ready to go anywhere near them. Holding her ground, the woman said, "Can I ask your name?"

"John Slocum," he replied absently. In the time it had

taken her to ask the question, his interest had already been captured by something lying nearby. He picked it up and tucked it into his pocket. Slocum then turned to find the woman staring at the fallen bushwhackers.

"I've . . . never really seen anything like this before," she said in a shaky voice. "Is . . . is that man shot?"

"Yes, but it's not bad. You might want to move along before one of them wakes up, though."

Slocum's point was made when the biggest man on the ground propped himself up and grunted as his bloody foot scraped against the dirt. The woman was quick to hop back and run away.

He rushed all the way to the opposite end of the alley and found exactly what he'd been expecting: nothing. Even if he hadn't bothered with the woman, Slocum knew there wasn't much of a chance of catching up with the third bushwhacker. That little weasel was too damn quick on his feet and Slocum was too sluggish on his. There may have been tracks in the alley, but Slocum didn't have a hope in hell of finding them in the inky darkness. Right now, all he wanted was to drag his sorry hide back down the street to the hotel where he was renting a room.

When he stepped onto the crooked boardwalk running alongside the street, Slocum bumped his toe against the warped wooden planks.

It took him a few tries to ease the Remington back into its holster after repeatedly catching the barrel on its worn leather.

Sweat rolled down Slocum's face to drip into his eyes. Or perhaps it was blood. Whatever it was, Slocum swiped at it with the back of one hand. He couldn't get much of a look at it because his vision was still blurred. Just as he was about to stumble again, he was caught by a steadying hand.

"Easy there," the woman in the flowered dress told him as she did her best to support his weight. "Let's get you somewhere you can sit down."

"What? I . . ."

"Don't try to talk," she said. "Save your breath."

Slocum's first instinct was to protest, but he couldn't quite get the words out. It turned out she was right. He really didn't have much breath to spare.

2

Slocum didn't exactly keel over, but he was a far cry from steady on his feet. He staggered like a drunk instead of falling face first onto the street thanks to the concerted efforts of the young woman who'd quite literally taken him under her wing. Although he didn't slip into unconsciousness, he somehow kept one foot shuffling in front of the other. Slocum felt like a tired spectator watching through the clouded windows of his own eyes. Every now and then, the sights and sounds surrounding him would dim before coming back to him in a rush.

Eventually, he was lowered onto his back with something soft beneath him. Slocum had no idea where he was, but he'd stopped moving, which was enough at the moment. After remaining motionless for several breaths, the contents of his stomach finally stopped sloshing inside him and splashing up to the back of his throat.

"Here," the woman said softly. "This should help."

Cool water splashed onto Slocum's forehead. It didn't

just feel good; it was the best damn thing he could imagine.

"Is that better?" she asked.

"Yes."

"I probably should have asked before dragging you away like that. It just seemed like the right thing to do. Should I have?"

"Yes," Slocum groaned. "You're a damn angel."

"Ummm . . . well . . . thank you. I think."

He blinked a few times to clear some of the cobwebs from behind his eyes. Although Slocum still couldn't see clearly, he could make out a bit more than he could a few seconds ago. The face looking down at him was pale and narrow. The woman had high cheekbones, a small mouth, and a nose with a distinctive upward slant. When he spoke again, Slocum could barely recognize the scratchy croak that emerged from his own mouth. "Got any more of that water?" he asked.

"Of course."

Seconds later, more was dripped onto his forehead and dabbed onto his cheeks. Just as Slocum was letting out a contented sigh, he felt a wet, cold blade poke into the top of his head. "Son of a bastard!" he growled while reflexively swatting at whatever had caused that sudden jab of pain.

Instead of anything resembling a weapon, the only thing Slocum found was the same rag that had brought him such bliss only moments ago. The woman pulled her hand back and recoiled after getting her wrist slapped. Slocum touched the throbbing portion of his scalp and was instantly reminded of the knock he'd taken shortly after leaving the saloon. His hand came away wet, but not from blood. Looking over, he could see the water-soaked rag dangling from her hand. "Sorry about that," he said.

She shrugged. "It's all right. I imagine that stung a bit."

"You could say that." He touched his tender scalp once more while asking, "Does it look bad?"

"It could use some cleaning, but it's not terrible. Usually when someone gets hit on the head, it bleeds a whole lot. You're already healing up. Must be because you're so strong."

"Nah," Slocum replied. "I just take more hits to the head than most folks. Where am I, by the way?"

"I brought you back to my house. It's not far from where you were attacked. Just at the far end of Hyde Street."

Slocum had seen a few modest homes in that direction but hadn't had cause to visit any of them. Pico Alto was a very small town but so far he'd only seen a sliver of it. In fact, he'd really only walked between his hotel, the Sunset Saloon, and one particular steak house so many times that he could have worn a rut in the ground. "I appreciate the kindness," he said while struggling to sit up, "but I won't impose any further. Just point me in the direction of Third Street and I can make my way back to my hotel."

"Which hotel? The One River?"

"That's it."

She shook her head so quickly that some of her hair fell across her face. "I can't allow that," she said while sweeping some of the longer strands behind one ear.

"You can't allow it?"

"That's too far for you to walk and you're not about to ride."

"Ride?" Slocum snapped as he sat up. "Why would I have to ride such a short . . . way . . . ?"

As things got blurry again, the only thing Slocum could see clearly was the smug grin on the woman's face. "See?" she said. "Just like I told you. You're not going anywhere."

Slocum pressed a hand to his head. It wasn't enough to

stop it from spinning, but at least he managed to slow it down a bit. "Guess I am still feeling shaky after taking that bump to the head."

"From the looks of it," she said while leaning forward to get a closer look at Slocum's scalp, "it seems like you took a lot more than a bump. Why don't you lay back down and I'll get your boots off?"

Even though he didn't seem capable of doing much else, Slocum acted as though he was making a concession when he stretched out and propped his feet onto the cot. Until that moment, he'd barely even taken much notice of his surroundings or where he'd been lying. It felt best when he kept his eyes shut, so he used both hands to feel the blankets beneath him. They were made from coarse wool and smelled of starch. Beneath them was nothing more than canvas stretched across a wooden frame.

"Are you all right?" she asked. "You're losing your color."

Slocum assured her that he was fine. Then he asked for her name. When she didn't answer, he realized he'd only thought those things and hadn't spoken a word. When he tried to sit up again, everything went black.

He awoke to a blinding light. Slocum lifted his hand to shade his eyes before opening them. At first, he couldn't see a thing. Then the fog cleared and he could see clearer than before he'd downed his first glass of whiskey the night before.

The light that had caused him to stir was merely a beam of sunlight sneaking in between the slats of shutters on the window closest to where he'd passed out. It took a few seconds to acclimate himself, but the rays were coming at such an angle that put the time at either dawn or dusk.

Slocum propped himself up on his elbows and waited

for the dizziness to return. When it didn't, he started digging into his pockets. There was nothing to find in there apart from a few loose threads and thirty-five cents.

"What can I get for you?"

Turning toward the familiar voice, Slocum found the woman with the pale skin and upturned nose. "I . . . can't find my watch."

"It's not there," she replied.

"Did you take it?"

She blinked. "No. I didn't take anything from you. If you can't find it, it must not be there. You were robbed last night. Don't you remember?"

Slocum sat up the rest of the way and swung his feet over the side of the cot. "I remember," he said while touching the tender spot on his head. There was a hell of a lump there and a gash covered in a crust of dried blood. Other than that, the light-headedness and other effects from the blow to the head seemed to have passed. He looked up at her, noticing plenty more than he had the night before.

For one thing, there was more light in the room now so he could see the smooth lines of her face. Although the woman's features were sharp, they were still very pretty. Her hair was tied back and tucked neatly beneath a plain white kerchief. Soft green eyes stared down at him, and thin red lips curled into a smile. "You really are feeling better," she said. "Before, you couldn't look at me this long without falling over. I hope that wasn't just because of how dreadful I looked when I found you."

"That's not it at all. I was out of my head."

"And what about now?"

Slocum placed his hand flat upon his forehead, slowly moved it back, and then let out a deep breath. "I'd say I'm mostly better. At least, I should be able to walk out of here on my own steam."

When he started getting up, the woman rushed forward to take hold of his arm so she could help support him. As much as Slocum wanted to refuse her assistance, he swallowed his pride and allowed her to see him to his feet.

"There!" she said triumphantly. "Much better. How's that?"

"Good." Once again focusing on her, he added, "I never did catch your name."

"You don't recall that either?"

"Recall what?"

"We had a conversation about an hour or so ago," she told him. "We introduced ourselves and you told me . . . well . . ." She smirked and looked away with mild embarrassment. "You said a few things that surprised me, but now I see you were probably just talking in your sleep."

"Yeah. I guess it was something like that. How long have I been on that cot?"

"Since last night."

Slocum let out a breath, relieved that he hadn't been out of sorts for much longer than that. He'd known of men who took knocks to the head and were on their backs for days at a stretch. "Since I don't recall what I spouted on about before," he said, "let's run through the introductions again. I'm John Slocum."

She smiled. "Kelly Thompson."

"I appreciate your hospitality, Kelly, but I won't impose on you any longer. Is there anything I can do to repay your kindness?"

"Don't worry about that. Also, you don't exactly have the means to pay for anything."

"You've got me there. Still, I won't forget about this. If there's anything you need, just let me know."

She stepped up to him and gently tugged at his shirt

collar. Instead of straightening it, she seemed more interested in finding an excuse to get as close to him as possible. "I'll do that, John."

For a moment, he thought she might take it a little further than that. However, she stepped back and picked up a faded handbag that had been lying on the floor. Kelly then walked over to a door at the back of the room and opened it. Instead of leading to another room, the door opened directly to the outside. She stepped through and shut it behind her.

Slocum opened another door that was closer to him and found that one led outside as well. What he'd previously thought was a small house was actually an even smaller cabin. The room where he'd spent the night was the only one there was, and Slocum turned around to get another look at it. In his clouded memories from the previous night, he couldn't recall much of anything apart from the cot, a few chairs, and a table. As it turned out, the only thing he'd overlooked was a little chest at the foot of the cot. Now that he examined them, the sparse, neatly arranged furnishings reminded him of a soldier's barracks. Rather than spending any more time thinking about the cabin, he put it behind him and headed for the street.

He'd forgotten to ask Kelly the time of day when she had still been around, but Slocum quickly pieced together that it was midmorning. It was a hazy day and felt like it would swiftly turn into a scalding afternoon. There was something unmistakable in the desert air that scraped against a man's skin until it felt more like the sand-blasted surface of sun-baked rock. When the desert sank its claws in too deep before noon, that meant it was going to be miserably hot. It hadn't taken many rides through Nevada for Slocum to figure that out for himself. This was the first time he'd visited this particular patch of the state, and judging by what he'd experienced so far, he hoped it would be the last.

Hyde Street was one of the main thoroughfares in Pico Alto. Dale Avenue was the other and both of those were divvied up by cross streets numbered one through four. Slocum's hotel was the One River on Third Street between the two main roads. He walked straight past the Sunset Saloon, doing his best to ignore the smell of stale beer and cigar smoke wafting from inside. Although he was feeling much better than before, his stomach was still churning in a most uncomfortable way beneath his rumpled shirt. His head ached just as he would expect after a night of drinking, and even though there weren't an unusual number of folks walking about, the sounds of their steps and voices were enough to make his eyeballs rattle. Of course, if he turned his head quickly enough, he could get the same result. Slocum decided to keep his movements slow and steady and ignore the noises around him as best he could.

The One River Hotel was a narrow building with three floors and only five rooms for rent. Slocum's was Room 2 and he was already dreading the walk up the single flight of stairs to get there. When he stepped through the front door, the first thing he saw was the tall beanpole of a man standing behind the front desk.

"Hello there, Mr. Slocum," the clerk said. "I didn't see you leave your room this morning."

"That's because I wasn't in my room," Slocum replied.

"Oh," the clerk said with a lewd grin. "I see. Well done."

Ignoring the clerk and the implications behind his comments, Slocum started climbing the stairs. He made it all the way to the fourth one before he stopped and patted his pockets. Letting out a pained breath, he turned around and climbed back down to the lobby.

"Hello again, Mr. Slocum," the clerk said without missing a beat. "Out for more carousing?"

"I don't have my room key."

"Did you misplace it while you were . . . you know . . . ?"

"I was robbed," he said.

Clearly disappointed by the explanation he'd gotten, the clerk took a moment to clear whatever thoughts were still teasing him from the aroused portion of his brain. "Robbed? Oh my. That's terrible."

"Yes, well, they got everything."

"Not your pistol."

"Look, I wasn't with a woman last night," Slocum snapped. "Save the jokes as well as the leering glances."

"No," the clerk quickly said. "I didn't mean *that* pistol. I meant the one right there."

When the clerk pointed at him, Slocum instinctively reached for the holster that was almost always at his side. It was still there and the Remington was still inside. Suddenly, a few more memories from the night before rushed through his head. The one that struck him in particular was when he'd been facing two of the bushwhackers and accidentally found the third one sneaking up behind him. It was then that he realized his pockets had been picked by someone who was very good at his job.

"Son of a bitch," Slocum growled.

"Pardon me?" the clerk said uneasily.

Turning an angry glare toward the tall man, Slocum said, "Look, it doesn't matter how my key was taken from me. My room is paid up through tomorrow and I need to get inside it. If there's a fee to replace the damn key, then tack it onto my bill."

The clerk held up his hands in a placating gesture. "No need to get all riled up. I was just making conversation is all. I'll get that key." He stooped down, dug through a drawer behind the desk, and quickly produced a key. Handing it over, he asked, "Anything else I can do for you?"

"No," Slocum replied as he snatched the key from him. "Did anyone come looking for me while I was gone?"

"No, sir."

Slocum was halfway up the stairs by now and completed his ascent without another word. When he got to his door, he stopped to place his hand upon the holstered .45. He tried the door, found it locked, and used the key to open it. Rather than stepping inside, he shoved the door open while drawing his pistol. By the time the door smacked against the wall and wobbled back, he had the Remington aimed at the narrow bed, which took up most of the space inside the rented room.

At first glance, everything seemed to be just as he'd left it. The bed was slightly rumpled. The basin on the table in the corner was half-full of water. Even his dirty clothes were piled right where they should have been. It took less than a minute to examine the rest of the room. Finally, Slocum sat on the bed, leaned forward, and felt beneath the bed for the saddlebags that had been folded flat and stored for safekeeping.

His fingers found the brushed leather, but couldn't get a grip right away. Usually he kept his saddlebags where he could see them—either draped over a chair or even propped in a corner. This time, they contained more than spare shirts and beef jerky so they'd been tucked away with a bit more care. He'd even stashed them so he could grab them quickly if he needed to get out of there in a hurry, which was how he knew for certain that somehow the bags had been turned around recently.

Slocum's teeth ground together as he pulled the bags out where he could see them. Whoever had gone through his belongings hadn't bothered to put them all back very carefully, because the buckle was undone and the cover was still open. He could tell the bags were light before opening them, and sure enough, the only thing left inside was a bundle of beef jerky that had been in there for at least a month. That meant his spyglass, compass, and other personal things were gone. More important, the bundle of cash totaling over three hundred dollars was gone as well. Slocum cursed under his breath. He reached all the way to the bottom of the saddlebag to place his hand flat against the side that faced the horse when they were being carried across its back. With a little searching, he found the spot where a hidden flap was tucked into a seam so it could go unseen by the casual eye. The flap came up and Slocum let out the breath he'd been holding when he felt the flat bundle of folded papers contained within the hidden space.

"Thank God," he sighed.

All things considered, his day could have gone a whole lot worse.

3

It was about a day and a half's ride south to the town of Genoa. Normally, Slocum wouldn't have climbed into his saddle so soon after taking such a knock to the head, but there was important business that needed to be conducted. Also, he knew he would feel better as soon as he put the town of Pico Alto to his back. In that respect, he was right. To be on the safe side, however, Slocum didn't leave town until late afternoon once he was certain he wouldn't pass out while in the saddle. His head was clear by then and improved even more once the crisp desert air started rushing by and his horse built up a good head of steam.

He spent that night stretched out on his back with a nice little fire crackling beneath a pot of beans and the stars splayed overhead. When he woke up the next morning, Slocum couldn't have felt any better. Any time he may have allowed to slip by thanks to the embarrassing turn of events in Pico Alto was made up when he blazed across the remaining trail leading into Genoa.

That town wasn't as large as some, but was a thriving place for business. There were plenty of stores, stables, and traders to be found as well as a whole lot of Mormons. Slocum didn't have anything against the Mormons as such. The only reason he noticed them at all was because a bunch of them were gathered for a shindig outside a trading post in the oldest section of town. There was a banner stretched across the street that said, WELCOME TO MORMON STATION, and a few clusters of folks talking about something or other. Slocum could have gotten more details about the gathering if he had stopped to ask any of the people there, but he didn't have the time.

The business that had brought him into Nevada in the first place was set to be wrapped up at another trading post down the street. After that, Slocum had every intention of continuing west into California. Genoa was less than twenty miles from the state line, and Slocum could damn near smell the salty San Francisco air blowing in from the Pacific. Even thinking along those lines for a few seconds was enough to get him feeling anxious. Slocum flicked his reins, nodded to one of the folks standing nearby, and made plans for how he would spend the rest of the money he was about to collect.

The trading post at the end of Slocum's ride wasn't one of the largest in town. It wasn't even close to being one of the most prosperous. As far as he could tell, the only reason it was still there at all was to host meetings like the one that had brought him into Genoa in the first place. The man who owned the property sat in a rocker outside his front door as though even he didn't expect any customers to sample his wares. He kept his hands folded across his wide belly and watched Slocum tie his horse next to two others drinking from a long trough. "Store's closed," the man grunted.

Patting his horse on the side of its neck, Slocum said, "I'm not here to shop."

"You got an appointment?"

"Yes," Slocum replied as he removed the saddlebags from the horse's back so he could drape them over his shoulder. "With Captain Vicker."

The fat man in the chair shifted his weight, but looked more like he was trying to get back to sleep instead of getting up. "You're s'pposed to leave your guns with me."

"Yeah? What happens if I resist?"

"Then you can take your chances with the fellas in the back room. I'm barely gettin' paid well enough to be a lookout."

Always more comfortable when heeled, Slocum tipped his hat to the man in front of the store and stepped inside.

It turned out that the sleepy fat man wasn't the only line of defense. The store itself consisted of one long aisle formed by two shelves that went from floor to ceiling, a couple of long tables, and one short counter with an old cash register on it. Two men wearing the blue uniforms of federal soldiers stood midway down the aisle. Each of them carried his rifle with the bayonet already fixed. By the time Slocum had taken two steps inside and the front door had swung shut behind him, both of those bayonets were pointed in his direction.

"Halt," the soldier on the right said sharply. "State your business."

"My name's John Slocum," he said while raising his hands so both soldiers could see them clearly. "My business is with Captain Vicker."

"What's the password?"

"Password?" Suddenly Slocum got the sneaking suspicion that he might have lost a thing or two when getting knocked in the head after all. After a few seconds, he said,

"Shit, I don't recall being given a password. How about you just get the captain so he can vouch for me?"

The soldiers remained silent and brought their rifles to their shoulders. "We can't let spies nor saboteurs speak a word to anyone that the Army was here," said the second uniformed man, who looked as deadly serious as the first. "Step away from that shelf so we don't damage any of this man's merchandise."

"What?"

"You heard him!" the first soldier barked. When Slocum opened his mouth to protest again, the soldier said, "Ready . . ."

"I was hit on the head! I don't remember any—"

"Aim!"

"For Christ's sake! I . . ."

"Stand down!"

That last order had come from someone other than the two soldiers standing guard in the store, but Slocum couldn't see anyone else step into the room, since his eyes had clamped shut. He didn't need to see, however, to know who it was. Keeping his eyes closed, Slocum let out a breath and lowered his hands. "Tom, I swear I'm going to kill you," he growled.

"Kill me? But I just saved your life!"

Slocum opened his eyes to find a third man in uniform standing between the first two. He had a youthful face that appeared even more so thanks to the wide smile plastered beneath his well-trimmed mustache. Even though the first two soldiers still had their rifles in firing position, both of them were smirking as well.

Shaking his head, Slocum removed his hat and used it to wipe some sweat from his brow. "That was a hell of a thing to do, Tom."

The youthful soldier strode past the other two, slapping

down the rifles as if they were nothing but children's toys. "After what you pulled in Carson City, I owed you one. It's a mighty fine feather in my cap to make John Slocum sweat."

"This wasn't from you," Slocum said as he flicked away one last bead running down his temple. "It's the damn heat. Are you gonna offer me some water, or do you still have an Apache raid to stage for my benefit?"

Still laughing, Tom walked up to Slocum and offered his hand. Grudgingly, Slocum shook it. "Got knocked on the head, huh?" Tom chuckled. "You used to bluff better than that."

"It's true." Slocum turned his head to display the spot on his scalp where a crust of blood had dried into his hair.

Tom examined the wound with all the care he might show to a rotten melon. "I'll be damned."

"Sergeant?" one of the soldiers in the makeshift firing line said. "The captain wants us to keep this area clear."

"Right, right. C'mon, John. Let's clear this area so these good men won't get into any trouble."

Placing his hat back onto his head, Slocum followed Tom toward a door at the back of the room. As he passed the two guards, he got apologetic shrugs from both of them. Slocum let out a tired laugh in return to let them know there were no hard feelings.

"So what's the goddamn password?" Slocum asked.

Tom draped an arm around Slocum's shoulders and shook him. "There is no password, you fool! Christ Almighty, you really did get some sense knocked out of you."

By now, they'd stepped through the door and into a cramped space that was part stockroom and part office. The storage part was filled with stacks of crates, piles of flour sacks, and random pieces of merchandise from the store shelves. Two uniformed guards stood at attention with their backs against the crates and rifles pressed close to their sides. One more soldier stood in the office portion of the room, where a stoop-shouldered man with thick dark hair and pale skin sat at the shopkeeper's desk examining a stack of papers.

"He's here, Captain," Tom announced.

"Who's that, Sergeant Graves?" the stoop-shouldered man asked. "Couldn't be our courier. He's supposed to be one of the best we could find. Surely he's not the kind to be so late for no good reason."

Slocum had only dealt directly with Captain Vicker once before. His first impression hadn't been anything close to good and wasn't about to improve anytime soon. Vicker's face was covered in a sheen of sweat just as it had been when Slocum met with him some time ago in a much cooler climate. His dark eyes were sharp and always narrowed as if he was constantly evaluating whoever stood in front of him. Now he didn't even bother turning those eyes toward Slocum.

"He ran into some trouble, sir," Tom said. "Took a blow to the head."

Captain Vicker finally twisted around in his chair to scowl up at Slocum. "Someone found out what you were carrying?"

Shaking his head, Slocum replied, "Not hardly. Just some cowardly robbers who got a lucky shot when my back was turned." Seeing the skepticism on Vicker's face, Slocum removed his hat to point at his messy wound. "Take a look for yourself if you don't believe me!"

"You're certain these robbers didn't know about your parcel?" Vicker asked.

"Yeah. All they got was my money, my watch, and . . ."

"And?"

Looking at the captain's sweaty face and being on the receiving end of Vicker's condescending stare, Slocum suddenly didn't feel very forthcoming. "And nothing. I checked right away and your precious parcel was right where it should be. Here," Slocum said as he slid the saddlebags from his shoulder and dropped them onto the floor near the desk. "See for yourself."

Vicker stood and straightened his starched white shirt. His nostrils flared as he approached Slocum without casting so much as a glance at the saddlebags. "You forget yourself, sir. You were commissioned for a job and to do it promptly."

"I'm here, ain't I?"

"You were supposed to be here yesterday at the latest."

"I told you why I was late."

"I don't care about your excuses," Vicker said. "If you were one of the men under my command, I'd have you thrown into the stockade for shirking your duty and behaving in such a belligerent manner."

"Well then," Slocum replied with a smug grin that he knew would get under the captain's skin, "it's a good thing I'm not under your command, now, isn't it?"

"For your sake . . . it certainly is." Glancing down at the saddlebags, Vicker asked, "That's the equipment you were issued in Carson City?"

"The same."

Vicker picked up the saddlebags, laid them out on top of the desk, and proceeded to unbuckle one side. He found the hidden flap after a small amount of searching, opened it, and removed the bundle of papers. He sifted through them, fretted a bit, and then sifted through them again. "These have been tampered with."

"I told you, I examined the bundle to make sure it was still in order," Slocum explained.

"And you were the only one to do so?"

"Far as I know, I'm the only one who knew there was anything but common supplies in those bags."

"Is that a fact?"

"Yes!"

Holding out the papers that had been stashed in the saddlebag as if he were displaying a winning poker hand, Vicker declared, "Then how do you account for this?"

Slocum looked at the papers and saw the same thing the last time he'd looked at them: a bunch of letters written in a neat script, none of which formed any words that made the first bit of sense. "I don't account for it at all," he said. "Looks like a bunch of nonsense to me."

"That's because it's in code."

"Well . . . good for you and your codes. I was just supposed to get those papers from one spot to another. You hired me because I could get the job done and handle myself without the need of any soldiers behind me if things got bad. Well, things did get a little rough but I handled it! If you wanted someone to translate your goddamn code, then you should've hired someone else."

Vicker stalked forward and lowered the papers so he could sneer directly into Slocum's face. "You were told not to disturb these papers at all."

"I wanted to make sure they were still there. If they weren't, I was ready to burn through hell and back to retrieve them."

"Is that supposed to excuse what happened, soldier?"

"I'm not one of your soldiers!" Looking over to the only other soldier in the room who wasn't just a guard, Slocum said, "I don't know what the hell is going on here!"

Tom nodded and placed a hand on Slocum's shoulder so he could move him back a step from Vicker. "All due respect, sir," Tom said, "but I'm inclined to agree. John didn't do anything wrong. He was attacked and he made certain his cargo was intact. I'm sure he didn't check it where anyone could see."

"I sure as hell didn't," Slocum said.

"If you took so many precautions," Vicker said, "then why is one page missing from this report?"

"A page is missing?" Slocum asked.

Vicker nodded. "Indeed it is. If you do not return it, I can safely assume you were responsible for taking it. That is treason, sir, and I can shoot you for that right here and now."

4

The soldiers in the room tightened their grips on their rifles.

Slocum turned very carefully to Tom and said, "Please tell me this is another one of your bad jokes."

"This is ridiculous!" Tom said. As soon as he saw the fire in Vicker's eyes, he added, "Captain . . . sir . . . if John wanted to commit treason, he wouldn't come here to meet with us only a little late for the appointment and stand among a group of armed men."

"Perhaps," Vicker said. "But that doesn't make the rest of this report appear in my hand."

"Did you check the other saddlebag?" Slocum asked.

"You told me you only inspected the papers once before putting them back."

"That's right, but the least you can do before executing me is to check the damn bags!"

"Corporal," Vicker said to the soldier closest to him, "if this man makes a move for the door . . . shoot him."

"Yes sir."

"You don't want to do this," Slocum warned. Shifting his eyes toward the soldier who'd gotten the order, he added, "And neither do you."

When Tom spoke again, it was with enough authority to make everyone in the room take heed. "John, shut up and stand still. Captain, search the rest of those bags before anyone does anything they'll regret."

Although he clearly didn't like taking orders instead of giving them, Captain Vicker carefully picked through the rest of the saddlebags. There hadn't been much inside them when Slocum had ridden from Pico Alto, and there was even less inside them now. Finishing his examination, Vicker discarded the bags as if they'd insulted every last one of his senses. "Nothing else is in there, Sergeant. Now what would you suggest?"

"There must be an explanation," Tom said. "I've known John Slocum long enough to know he ain't no spy."

"Of course I'm not," Slocum snapped.

"Then what happened to my missing page?" Vicker asked.

"Are you certain there was another page?"

The captain's voice was cold as ice when he said, "I can decipher this report and there *is another page*."

"All right, then," Slocum said. Knowing how careful he'd been with the saddlebags ever since he'd been given this job, he could only think of one possible explanation. He wasn't one for lying if there was any way around it, but if he wanted to prevent Captain Vicker from completely losing what was left of his temper, a small untruth of the white variety was in order. "I think I know what happened here," he said.

Not ready to be consoled just yet, Vicker said, "Tell me."

"It's probably back at the hotel where I was staying."

"Why would it be there? Are you saying there's a chance one of those robbers has it?"

"What I'm saying is that . . . I may have hidden it somewhere on my own when I was staying there."

"Why would you remove the bundle from the secure compartment of the equipment you were issued?" Vicker asked through clenched teeth.

"Because, no matter what fancy names you have for it, that equipment is still just a pair of saddlebags and the secure compartment is still a leather flap. You hired me to make certain those papers stayed safe and I thought they'd be safer if they weren't always kept beneath a leather flap in a saddlebag."

Vicker's tone was as sharp as it was icy when he said, "That seemed to work out real well."

"When I transferred them from one spot to another, I must have left one behind."

"Which means you must have seen the contents."

"Ain't that why it's coded?" Slocum asked. "I watched the major who had the papers to begin with wrap that bundle myself right before he stuck it under that flap when I started this job. I saw as much then as I did any other time. There wasn't one of them times that any of that writing looked like anything but a bunch of nonsense."

Vicker placed the papers he did have on the desk, spread them out, and bowed his head. "Can you get the missing page back or not?"

"I can."

"I want it by tomorrow."

"Then give me a horse that can fly," Slocum replied.

"I'll give you three days, then," the captain told him. "Any longer than that and I'll start deducting from the remainder of the money you're owed for completing this job."

"Come on now, Captain," Tom said. "You knew there would be risks involved. That's why we hired John to ride without drawing any attention. Hell, that's why we didn't use anyone in the Army for that matter. Any job with risks probably won't run on schedule."

"I know all of that, Sergeant," Vicker replied evenly. "That's why I haven't had Mr. Slocum here shot or put into irons for making such a mess of this particular job."

Slocum wanted to argue, but knew the officer had a point.

"Get me my missing page," Vicker said. "Or the least of your worries will be returning the first half of that money you were given."

"Speaking of money," Slocum said. "I am going to need a small advance on the rest of my pay."

The guards tensed in preparation for the storm they were fully expecting to come.

"I've got to hand it to you, Slocum," Vicker said in a quiet voice that didn't make the guards around him feel any better. "When Sergeant Graves recommended you, he told me you had real sand. Asking me for more money after what's already happened on your watch . . . well, that proves he was right."

"I'm not trying to give you any grief, Captain," Slocum said. "The men who gave me this," he explained while pointing to the messy gash on his head, "also took my money. I'll need some more for expenses and such. That's all."

"Funds that would normally be requisitioned and allotted to you by the government are now coming out of your own pay."

"That's the idea."

Vicker nodded once. "I'll see to it. Anything else?"

Although he wasn't threatened by the officer, Slocum also wasn't about to press his luck with the man. He kept his voice and demeanor respectful without licking any boots when he said, "I'll bring your page back to you. Just give me enough time to do it without breathing down my neck or calling in a bunch of men that will send the robbers into the hills."

"I'll trust your judgment on this," Vicker replied. Quickly, he lifted a finger and added, "But I will not abide any more failure on your part. If that page isn't found, I'll take you into custody. If you try to run from me, I'll make it my personal mission to rip this country apart until I track you down. A man like you can't stay hidden for long."

"Believe me," Slocum chuckled, "I'm well aware of that."

"Good. Now get out of my sight and do your damn job."

Slocum felt a twitch. Before he could act on it, Sergeant Graves took hold of his arm and led him toward the door. "Come on, John," he said. "Let's get some fresh air."

By the time he was escorted through the main part of the store and shown outside, Slocum could have ground a piece of coal between his teeth until it became a diamond. His breaths were short and shallow. His heart thumped within his ribs like a caged animal.

"Thought I'd get you out of there before you took a swing at the captain," Tom said.

"You tellin' me you wouldn't have approved?" Slocum asked.

"Can't say I haven't thought of it a time or two myself, but you know damn well it's a bad idea."

After a long exhale, Slocum said, "I guess you're right. Don't mean I gotta be happy about it."

"See this uniform?" Tom asked while brushing the back of one hand against his dark blue jacket as if he were trying to sell it to a customer.

"Yeah."

"This uniform means I make my living off of doing one thing after another that I'm not happy about."

Slocum couldn't help smiling at that. Now that his anger had passed, Slocum took a look around to see he'd been taken all the way past the front of the store to stand somewhere that the fat man in the chair outside couldn't listen in on them. "All right," Slocum said. "I got my wits about me so I won't take a swing at your commanding officer. Not yet anyway."

"If you do get around to it," Tom said, "make sure I'm there to see it. At least we'll have something to talk about when you're in the stockade."

"Just me? I'll make certain Vicker knows it was your idea for me to knock his head from his shoulders."

Now that he was able to see the small lot behind the store, Slocum spotted where the rest of the horses were tethered. There was also a small carriage that was undoubtedly Vicker's. "So what the hell is in those reports that's so damn important anyway?"

Tom shrugged. "I don't know. Ain't my job to know."

Slocum fished a dented cigarette case from his shirt pocket, opened it, took one for himself, and held the case toward Tom. "Must be something big."

Tom took a cigarette and lit it using a match Slocum had struck. "It is. I can guarantee it."

The light from the sputtering match cast a flickering glow onto Slocum's face as he brought it closer to ignite his cigarette. Smoke curled from the glowing ember as he flicked the match to the ground and stomped it out. "You never mentioned Captain Vicker before this job. What do you know about him?"

"You weren't so concerned when you took the advance pay," Tom pointed out.

"That's when I thought it was just a simple courier run."

"It still is. From what I heard, I'm guessing you got drunk at a saloon, stumbled down the wrong street, and got jumped by some assholes looking to make quick money. As for the page, you left it behind by accident, right?"

"What kind of a fool do you take me for?" Slocum growled.

"The kind that's not very good at lying to a friend."

After maintaining his grim facade for another second or two, Slocum let it drop and took a long pull from the cigarette. "I guess you're not too far off. But it wasn't like I was carrying those papers on me. They were kept safe and I stepped out to unwind a bit. Didn't think there was anything wrong with that. I had every intention of getting here on time."

"No need to convince me, John. I never thought you would allow anything like this to happen. It's just one of them turns of bad luck. Any man who's lived any kind of life has had more than a few of those."

"Some more than others. I'll start the ride back to Pico Alto soon as I'm through with this smoke," Slocum said. "That being said, there's a chance that the missing page wasn't just left behind. When I was being robbed, my pocket was picked. I wasn't carrying much, but they got my watch and . . ."

"Yeah?" Tom prodded.

"And . . . the key to my hotel room. They must have gotten into my room and taken everything else they could."

"That's how they got to all of your money?"

Slocum nodded.

"Shit," Tom grunted. "I knew you wouldn't carry the entire sum on you when you were drunk. There's gonna be hell to pay if the captain finds out you kept it from him."

"The only reason I didn't mention that was because the best way for this mess to be cleaned up is by me. I couldn't abide being told to walk away altogether. First, I'd like to know everything about what and who I'm dealing with. What kind of slack do you think I've got with the schedule I was given?"

Tom leaned out to get a better look at the front of the store. He then walked a short way along the side of the building so he could get a look at the back. Even though he was satisfied that no other Army men were out there with them, he dropped his voice to a whisper when he said, "Captain Vicker ain't one to say anything without meaning it."

"He'll toss me into the stockade if I'm late?" Slocum asked.

"As long as you get the job done, I'd say he'll be willing to bargain on that account. Just don't push him." A grin slipped onto his face as he added, "I was surprised as hell when you asked him for that money. Even more surprised when he agreed to give it to you."

Slocum drew some more smoke into his lungs and breathed it out. "That wasn't much of a gamble. If he wants the job done on any sort of schedule, anyone would need a few dollars to travel on."

"Still, not many men in uniform would've had the guts to ask for it." Lowering his voice until it almost couldn't be heard, Tom added, "Vicker is with the Military Intelligence Corps. Those men ain't the sort to be tested. Especially if they've risen to the rank of captain."

"I figured as much. Even though I wasn't of a mind to ask a whole lot of questions when I took the job, I thought I smelled something other than regular Army on that one."

"And you still took the job?"

"You vouched for him, Tom. I knew you wouldn't steer me wrong. Besides," he added while flicking his cigarette down and crushing it beneath his boot, "I needed the money."

"I just hope I didn't get you into some kind of mess."

"The mess is my fault. I'll set it right."

Reluctantly, Tom said, "I'm talking about the kind of mess that could get you hurt. Or worse."

"You sure there isn't anything more you want to tell me about those papers?"

"I know they're drawing enough heat from dangerous types for the captain to hire someone not connected to the Army to run them to where they needed to be."

"Which means he was expecting someone to take a run at them between Carson City and here," Slocum said. "This isn't the first time it's been safer for someone to make a delivery while the enemy wasn't looking. Of course, it would've helped if I'd known exactly how important those papers were."

Tom slowly shook his head. "I've been trying to figure out who is after those papers. All I got was the name *Shockley.* That mean anything to you?"

Slocum didn't have to think long before shaking his head and saying, "Nope."

"Just recently, Vicker started getting telegrams left and right about that delivery. Far as what's on them papers . . . you got me. Could be troop movements, news from the president . . . any number of things. I'm just guessing, though."

Patting Tom on the shoulder, Slocum said, "It's all right. No need to strain anything thinking too hard."

Tom swatted away Slocum's hand and chuckled, "Eh, to hell with you, John. Last time I try to do you any favors."

"If your favors all have these kinds of strings attached, you can keep 'em." Although he'd meant that as·a joke, Slocum immediately regretted saying it. Tom was still smiling, but a nerve had obviously been struck. Slocum quickly said, "I know you wouldn't put me in harm's way. You were just trying to help me out."

"I knew there was some risk, but I figured it wasn't anything you couldn't handle. The money was good and—"

"Stop it," Slocum said. "You didn't force me into anything. I barely heard three sentences out of Vicker before I took the job and his money. All I got was a knock on the head, and as far as that goes, you were right. I was drunk and probably made a stupid mistake or just stepped somewhere I shouldn't have. Either way, I should've heard someone comin'."

"Yeah, well, neither one of us knew the whole story going in. Now that we can see some more of the picture, I don't think you should go this one alone."

"Now more than before, I need to handle this on my own. If I move quickly, I should still be able to catch up to whoever took that page. Odds are they're just some local assholes who don't know what they've got. I've tracked down their kind more times than I can count. More than likely, they're still right there in town spending my money on whiskey and women. If I ride in there with an Army man at my side, they'll hole up somewhere and make it that much harder for me to flush them out."

"I don't have to wear the uniform, John."

"Tell you what," Slocum said. "If I need someone to watch my back, I'll send word straight to you. Otherwise, just keep Vicker happy and buy me some time."

"I can do that. Just do something for me."

"Name it."

"Try not to get yourself killed over a dumb mistake."

Slocum smiled. "It is bound to happen sooner or later."

5

The money Slocum was given had been requisitioned straight from the fat man's till. It was a good enough sum to see Slocum through, but judging by the amount of grumbling that came from the store's owner when he handed it over, it was a small fortune. Not wanting to waste any time on the matter, Slocum climbed right onto his horse and headed out of town. He rode as far as he could before the daylight dwindled to nothing and his animal was too tired to take another step. When he made camp, Slocum built a small fire and sat down to catch his breath. That was when he realized he hadn't taken the time to requisition himself any fresh supplies while he'd been in town.

"Damn," he grumbled as he stuck his hand into his saddle-bags. "Looks like that old jerky I've been carrying around will have to do."

Suddenly, Slocum was reminded of an old joke he'd heard about a cook on a wagon train who had good news and bad news. The bad news was that there were only moldy potatoes to eat. The good news was that there was plenty of 'em to go around. There was more jerky in that saddlebag than Slocum would have guessed, and he ate damn near all of it before stretching out and getting to sleep.

The next morning, he woke early and headed out in record time. Riding on an almost empty stomach drove him to keep forging ahead better than a set of spurs being dug into his sides. When he finally caught sight of Pico Alto, it was early evening. He almost hopped down from the saddle so he could run the rest of the way into the small town just to get a square meal into his belly. Since the One River Hotel had a small stable behind it, he went straight there, put up his horse, and ordered the biggest steak they could scrounge up. Being a hotel and not a steak house, his cut of beef was gristly and damn near charred to a crisp. But Slocum would have wolfed down a pile of wood chips if it was served to him, and he was more than grateful for what he got.

"Mr. Slocum?"

Slocum had seen the clerk walk into the hotel's cramped dining room, but didn't want to lift his head from his plate unless it was absolutely necessary. Since he only had a few more string beans left, he stabbed them with his fork and nodded at the man who'd checked him into his room a few minutes ago.

"A man was asking about you," the clerk said.

Squinting suspiciously, Slocum asked, "Someone knew I'd be coming back here?"

"No, no," the clerk quickly amended. "He was asking about you the other day, but it was after you'd checked out. He seemed quite interested in finding you."

"Yeah? Did he have a key to my room?"

Recoiling in surprise at hearing that question, the clerk

replied, "A key? No! He came to the front desk and asked for you by name."

"How did he know who I was?"

"I . . . I don't know."

"What did he want?"

Clearly flustered by the increasing tension in Slocum's voice, the clerk said, "He just came asking for you because he wanted to speak to you about something. At least . . . that's what I gathered. I told him you were checked out and that I had no idea where you . . . where you might have . . ."

"All right," Slocum said while pushing back from the table. "Didn't mean to rake you over the coals. Maybe he'll come back."

"I can send for him if you like."

"So you know who he was?"

The clerk collected himself and straightened the collar of his starched shirt even though it was plenty straight already. "I do know who he was. His name is Scott Jeffries and he lives not far from here. I was going to tell you as much before you . . . well . . . I suppose I got a little rattled."

"Happens to every man. Go ahead and send for him."

"That will be fine," the clerk said before drawing a few calming breaths. "I'll see to it personally. And as far as what you asked before, regarding him having a key to your room, I do remember something about that."

Slocum glared at the scrawnier man. "I also asked about that when I was here before."

"You did. It was when you were still so upset about what had happened."

When Slocum thought back to how he'd stormed into his hotel after being robbed and stormed back down the stairs again after realizing his saddlebags had been tampered with, the word *upset* didn't quite cover it. Rather than giving voice to that, he let the clerk continue.

"I try to commit all of my guests to memory," the clerk said. "That's how I provide such intimate service and make you feel at home here at the One River."

"Uh-huh."

"The man I saw on the night when you didn't return, well, he just walked right upstairs like he owned the place and I didn't even recognize him. He was a rather skinny fellow."

Slocum stood up and held a hand up to what he remembered to be the skinny bushwhacker's height. "About this tall?" he asked.

"Yes! Do you know him?"

"Did he go up to my room?"

"That's the thing," the clerk replied with a wince. "I'm not positively certain. I did ask the other guests and one of them thought she saw that skinny gentleman near your door."

"So he was either in my room or he just walked upstairs for no reason," Slocum said dryly.

Acting as if he'd experienced a revelation, the clerk said, "Exactly! Could have been nothing at all."

"Wonderful. Do me a favor and try to pay closer attention if someone other than me could be stepping into my room."

"Of course, sir," the clerk said, obviously missing the sarcasm dripping from Slocum's voice. "Anything else I can do for you?"

"No. That'll do it." Slocum handed over a small amount of the money he'd been given and said, "Have someone make sure my horse is properly fed and watered. I was in a bit of a rush when I got to town."

The clerk smiled and brought two fingers to his

forehead as if he was tapping the brim of a hat. Embracing the more familiar task he'd been given, he turned on his heels and rushed away to see it was done.

Slocum left the dining room as well and stepped out through the front door. Once outside, Slocum took a moment to get his bearings. Retracing his steps from when he'd been brought back to the hotel after leaving Kelly Thompson wasn't easy. His memories were still hazy, which made it difficult to recall anything from that night with any degree of accuracy. So instead of using memory, Slocum relied on his instinct and a bit of common sense.

First, he walked back to Hyde Street and the Sunset Saloon. As he got closer to that place, things started feeling more familiar. He found the spot where he'd been jumped. Slocum then headed in the direction his instincts pointed him and kept an open mind. Before long, the loose strategy paid off.

He made his way out of Pico Alto's saloon district, skirted the edge of a row of shops, and spotted a group of cabins that struck a very familiar chord. Try as he might, Slocum couldn't nail down which exact cabin had been Kelly's. Some movement caught his eye as one or two people flickered in and out of view while passing behind two of the little homes. The next thing he heard was a door opening and a surprised voice.

"John? Is that you?"

Kelly emerged from one of the cabins. She wore another simple dress, but one that was cut from cotton dyed a much darker color than what she'd had on before. Her hair wasn't tied back this time and fell around her face in layers of straight, dark red strands. Approaching her, Slocum said, "It sure is! I was hoping I'd find you." Despite the fog that had been in his head that other night, he remembered Kelly as a very attractive woman. Now that he was looking at her with clear eyes, he could tell his first impression had been dead on target.

"I thought you'd left town," she said.

He stepped a little closer. "I did," he told her. "But I came back."

The surprise that had been on her face quickly melted into a warm smile. "I'm glad. Want to come in for a spell?"

Slocum responded with actions instead of words, stepping past her to go inside the cabin. She was right behind him and closed the door partway before finally shutting it.

"Are you expecting someone?" he asked.

"No."

"Good." With that, he took hold of her by the arms so he could turn her to face him. She tensed for a moment, but didn't resist. When he leaned down to kiss her, Kelly's body was quick to react. In a matter of seconds, she'd melted against him.

"I . . . wasn't expecting this," she whispered.

"You seemed awfully close to me when I was here before," he pointed out. "Should I leave?"

"No."

"Then I'd like to thank you for helping me." Slocum kissed her again. His mouth lingered on hers and before long her lips parted to allow his tongue to slide between them. Once they'd gotten a good taste of each other, their bodies pressed together even harder and Kelly's arms wrapped around the back of Slocum's neck.

Her breath came in sharp gasps and caught in her throat when she felt his hands on her backside to cup her tight little ass. "I wasn't sure you had your eye on me," she whispered.

"Well . . . now you know." Slocum gathered up her skirts until he could feel the bare skin of her thigh. His hand wandered farther beneath her skirt and against her thighs until he could feel what was between them. She was wet and getting wetter by the second.

"Why are you . . . back in . . . back in town?" Kelly asked as his fingers ran along the smooth lips of her pussy.

Kissing her neck and then her ear, he said, "I was passing this way again and thought about you. Thought about this," he added while slipping a finger inside her.

Kelly gasped and leaned back as if she'd suddenly lost the strength to stand on her own. Her eyes were clenched shut, and when they opened again, there was a fresh spark in them. Now she reached down to undress him. Her hands found his belt buckle and unfastened it so she could shove his jeans down past his hips. His cock was already stiff and filled her hand as she started stroking him. "I've been thinking about this, too," she said. "When I took you in, I was hoping you'd wake up and thank me like this."

Slocum pulled her skirts all the way up around her waist and pulled aside the flimsy undergarment she wore. Gripping the leg she'd wrapped around his waist, he said, "How about you take me in right now?"

Kelly smiled, closed her eyes, and guided him between her legs so Slocum could bury his rigid pole all the way inside her. Both of them groaned loudly and stayed still for a few moments to savor what they were feeling. Then, keeping hold of one of her legs, he eased out of her and pumped in again. Kelly gripped his shoulders and leaned back as much as she could. Her back was against the wall beside the door and the cot was close enough for her to place a foot upon its frame for some measure of support. There wasn't much room to maneuver within the cabin, which didn't pose a problem at the moment. The only movement either of them wanted didn't involve them getting more than a few inches apart from each other.

Slocum pumped in and out of her in a building rhythm.

When he felt the end drawing near, he eased up for a moment so he could catch his breath. "Why did you stop?" she asked.

Still partially inside her, Slocum moved his hands along her hips and sides to draw her dress up along the way. The garment came all the way off with a little help from Kelly, exposing her firm, round breasts. They were on the small side, but contoured beautifully with little pink nipples that stood tall and erect. Her pearl-colored skin was coated in a fine sheen of sweat. Slocum cupped his hands beneath her ass, picked her up off the floor, and carried her the short distance to the cot. The instant he put her down again, Kelly sat on the edge of the cot and reached out to cup his manhood.

Her mouth wrapped around Slocum's thick member as she took him all the way in. He allowed her to suck on him for a few seconds, but soon pushed her back. Kelly looked up with wide eyes and asked, "Don't you like that?"

He didn't say a word. Instead, he pushed her back and then got her situated so her backside was perched upon the edge of the cot and her legs hung over the side. She was more than happy to let him place her where he wanted and then position himself between her legs. She opened them wide for him, lay back, and ran her hands along the front of her body. Slocum took her hips in his hands and lifted her lower body up just high enough to enter her again. As soon as the tip of his cock touched the pink lips between her thighs, Kelly wrapped her legs around him and held on tight.

Slocum gripped her in both hands, moving them so he could alternate between rubbing her hips and her taut little ass. Her pussy gripped him tightly as Slocum pumped in and out of her. Kelly closed her eyes, turned her head to breathe directly into her blanket, and ground her lower body against his.

He moved in and out of her, building momentum until their bodies pounded together and the cot creaked beneath her weight. Every time Slocum drove his cock into her, Kelly grunted and her muscles tensed. It wasn't long before her eyes snapped open and she became quiet. Next, she arched her back and tightened her grip on Slocum with her legs. At the last possible second, he used one hand to rub the sensitive flesh just above her opening. Almost immediately after the tip of his thumb found her clit, Kelly writhed in a powerful orgasm. She gritted her teeth and bucked against him, surprising even Slocum with how wild her reaction became.

Soon he felt his own climax approaching. He used both hands to pull her up tight against him and pounded into her again and again until the flood built up within him. After one more thrust, he exploded inside her while letting out a long, shuddering breath. He kept still for a few seconds before finally letting her go and taking a step back.

"That," she gasped. "That was . . ."

"Yeah," he said as he lowered himself onto the cot beside her. "It sure was."

There was still some sunlight coming in between the slats on one of the cabin's windows. Before long, it would be dark. Slocum and Kelly spent the next hour or so wearing each other out until both of them drifted off to sleep on the cot with nothing but a thin sheet to cover them.

6

Although he could have stayed asleep for a good deal longer, Slocum awoke before dawn. He slipped out from beneath the arm that Kelly had draped across his chest, pulled on his pants, and eased his gun belt around his waist. Every step of the way, he kept an eye on her to make certain she wasn't about to wake up and discover what he was up to. Not only did she continue to breathe heavily and steadily, but she also rolled onto her side so her back was to him.

Knowing he wouldn't have much time in which to work, Slocum started searching the cabin. Fortunately, there wasn't much to see. In a few short minutes, he'd looked through the obvious places. There was nothing but clothes in the little chest of drawers against one wall and only dust beneath the bed. A carpetbag sat in the corner next to the cot and Slocum sifted through that to find some dirty, rumpled clothes that struck him as awfully familiar. Having struck pay dirt, he dug a little deeper.

Instead of simply feeling inside the bag, Slocum ran his fingers along the inner seams. When he got to the bottom, he found the rigid piece used to keep the shape at the bottom of the bag. It seemed perfectly normal until he found one spot where the seam didn't quite hold as it should. He knew it was more than just an imperfection in the bag when he got one finger beneath the bottom piece and was able to pull the whole thing up. Beneath it was a small space where a few things could be wedged in between the false and real bottom, which was similar in design. In that space were a few folded dollars, some dirty clothes, a .38, and one last object that brought a smile to Slocum's face.

"What are you doing?"

Having heard the brush of movement behind him, Slocum wasn't too surprised to hear Kelly's voice. "I'm thanking my lucky stars for finding this," he told her.

"Finding what?"

Slocum picked up the object he'd found wrapped in a dirty old bandanna and held it up as he turned around to face her. The dented pocket watch dangled from his hand on its chain. Kelly stood beside the cot, wearing only the sweat that she and Slocum had worked up during their lovemaking. She gripped a Derringer in one hand.

"If I hadn't found this," Slocum said calmly, "I would've felt like a real bastard for rooting through your things this way."

"Is that what this is about?" she asked. "You're robbing me while I sleep?"

"I don't mind a little irony every now and then, but you can stop your accusations right there, lady. This here is *my* watch."

"Maybe you dropped it," she replied. "Just like you dropped all your other clothes not too long ago."

"Yeah," Slocum said. "I just dropped my watch, which I haven't seen since I was robbed, and it happened to land beneath the false bottom of your carpetbag. That sounds real likely."

"So this is why you came here?" Kelly asked with a sad pout. "You had your way with me just so you could search my things once my guard was down?"

Slocum tucked the watch away and kept his hand in his pocket for the moment. "I've been on the other end of that trick plenty of times. Thought I'd see what it's like to be the one with the advantage for a change. You know something? It's kind of nice."

"You smug bastard. Get out."

Slocum took a small, cautious step toward the door and stopped. "You in a hurry to be rid of me?"

"Would you rather I fetched the law?"

"You won't do that."

"Why not?" she asked.

"Because you'd be in just as much trouble as me. Once I had a chance to explain a thing or two . . . I imagine you'd be in a whole lot more trouble."

"For what?"

Slocum carefully picked up the rumpled bandanna that had been wrapped around the watch. "For this."

She smiled, but it was an expression that didn't seem very comfortable on her. "Should I be threatened by a dirty rag?"

"Not as such. You might be interested to know that I found this rag hidden away in the alley where I found you. It's the bandanna that was covering the face of one of the robbers who jumped me that night. The same one that picked my pocket."

"You were chasing that robber away," Kelly said. "Just

because he looked like he might have had a similar build as me, he was wrapped up in too many clothes for you to know for sure."

"That's what you were banking on. Isn't that right?" Slocum said.

"I was just trying to help you when you were wounded," Kelly told him in a trembling voice. "Then you come back here, take advantage of me, and try to rob me. Lord only knows what you intended on doing to me while I was asleep."

"Is that why you go to sleep with a gun in your hand?"

"I suppose you'd rather I allow you to take what you pleased," she replied.

"An innocent woman in your place might have just wanted to get away," he told her. "Instead, you decide to bare your teeth to defend one carpetbag. The only reason I can think of for that is you were worried I might piece together what I've already pieced together. You and those accomplices of yours were the ones who jumped me that night."

Kelly furrowed her brow as if she was hearing something that both shocked and scared her.

"After you picked my pocket," Slocum continued, "you took off running, ditched the clothes you wore to make you look like one of the robbers, and then attended to me."

"And if I was such a horrible person," she asked as if the very act of saying those words disgusted her, "why would I try to help you?"

Slocum merely shrugged. "Because you wanted to buy some time for the other two to escape. Perhaps you wanted to wait for a chance to finish me off after my guard was down."

"John! That's terrible!"

"Maybe you had other reasons," he said. "Maybe it was a little bit of all the ones I mentioned. Truth is, I don't care now that I know I'm right. These clothes," he told her while holding up the shirt that was kept hidden at the bottom of her carpetbag, "were the ones worn by the robber who picked my pocket. This is the bandanna that was ditched in the alley after I was robbed. I had it in my pocket when you brought me here the first time, and when I left, it was gone. You must've picked my pocket again and stashed the evidence away. You even got my watch and I suspect there's a stash of even more stolen property somewhere nearby."

Her attempt to look frightened, threatened, offended, or anything else along those lines was abandoned in favor of annoyance with a hint of curiosity. "You're the one who seems to know so damn much," Kelly said. "Why don't you tell me?"

"I've seen more than enough to know I'm right and you already know what you've done so I don't have to explain myself any further. Just show me the rest of what you stole."

Tightening her grip on the weapon she carried, Kelly stood up straight as if she wore a suit of armor instead of nothing at all. "You may have surprised me by coming back here and . . . doing what you did . . . but I'm still the one with the upper hand."

"Are you?"

She nodded. "I've got something you want." Arching her back a bit to display her pert breasts, she added, "Several things, as a matter of fact."

"The only thing you can offer that I can't get from a hundred other places is the rest of what you stole from me. Hand it over."

The fire that showed in her eyes this time around was clearly genuine. "You're the one who searched this cabin. You should know I'm not hiding anything else in here."

"Where, then?"

"Perhaps it would help if you told me what it is I'm supposed to have."

Showing no fear of the Derringer, Slocum placed his hand on the Remington. "I've had my fill of this bullshit. You know goddamn well what you stole. I want it back."

Kelly's eyebrows lifted as if she were watching a favored pet perform a new trick. "You'd shoot me? After what we've been through?"

"That sugar between your legs was sweet, I won't deny that. But it ain't enough to blind me to every other thing that's happened."

Glancing down at her own naked body, she whispered, "I wouldn't be so sure about that."

The walls of the cabin shook as the narrow back door was rattled on its hinges and forced open. The latch holding it in place snapped like it was made from paper, allowing the big bull of a man who'd faced Slocum on the night he was robbed to come charging inside.

Normally, Slocum wouldn't want to harm a woman when she stood naked in front of him. Kelly, however, had proven herself to be something more than the average woman. The weapon she held made her a target. He drew the Remington and lowered his aim for a wounding shot, but his effort at chivalry counted for nothing since the hammer of his pistol slapped against an empty cylinder.

"What the hell?" Slocum growled as he looked at the gun in his hand. His mind raced. He knew he'd checked the pistol more than once that day and couldn't come up with a definitive time when Kelly or anyone else could have emptied it. He must have fallen asleep a bit longer than he'd guessed, but none of that mattered. The only thing that did was that his gun was empty and those carried by his attackers, most likely, were not.

Less than a second had ticked by and the big man was still standing in the door. Kelly hadn't wasted a moment. While Slocum tried to fire at her, she'd launched herself at the carpetbag while retrieving a knife that had been hidden under her pillow. She snapped her left hand toward him and the blade flicked through the air, carving a small sliver from Slocum's calf. By the time he felt a biting jab of pain, she'd taken hold of the carpetbag's handle.

"Put him down, Connell!" she shouted on her way to the front door. "Then meet us at the edge of town!" With that, she threw open the door and bolted outside, naked as the day she was born.

Connell took up so much space in the cabin that the shotgun in his hands looked like a toy. Having spotted Slocum, he bared his teeth and brought the shotgun around to aim from the hip. Slocum swung his Remington to take aim, but wound up cracking it against the big man's fingers. While unexpected, the collision did knock the shotgun to one side as thunder erupted from its barrel.

The gunshot was deafening but didn't draw blood. Slocum's ears were ringing as he drove as many hard blows into Connell's midsection as he could. He used his fist and the empty pistol to thump against the big man's ribs like he was chopping into the trunk of a tree. When the shotgun's stock was swung at him in a short, clubbing arc, Slocum ducked beneath it and drove his shoulder into Connell's gut. Both men stumbled toward the back wall, shaking the entire cabin when Connell hit the flimsy wooden planks with his shoulders. Cheap, weathered wood gave way, allowing the two men to charge outside.

Fortunately, there was no raised porch at either end of

the cabin. That way, neither man had anywhere to fall after stumbling through the newly widened back door. Because Slocum was the one doing the pushing, he kept the larger man off his balance by keeping his legs churning against the ground like a pair of pistons moving an engine along a track. Before Connell got his wits about him, Slocum knocked the shotgun from the big man's grasp and put a little distance between them so he could renew his attack.

As Slocum chopped away at the man-shaped bull in front of him, he started to think he was gaining a genuine advantage. His left fist landed solidly and Connell grunted as it slammed against a tender portion of his torso. When the Remington was swung toward his chin, however, Connell swatted it aside with ease.

"That's enough of that," the big man grunted. Then he launched an attack of his own.

Slocum could see the punches coming, but the swings were so wild and Connell's fists were so wide that it was next to impossible to avoid them all. Connell was strong enough that even a glancing blow from him was enough to make Slocum sorry he'd gotten up that morning. When Slocum attempted to use his arms to block a punch, all he got was a pair of bruised arms. Connell clasped his hands together and raised both fists in the air as if he was about to drive an axe blade into the ground. Slocum swung upward to hit Connell's elbow to divert the big man's swing and avoided it with a shuffling sidestep. Before he could celebrate the small victory, Slocum felt two large palms slap against his shoulders like a pair of meaty frying pans. He was then lifted off his feet and tossed to the ground. Before Slocum could get up, Connell came at him with a punch that was surely going to send him into next week.

"Stop right there!" someone shouted from behind Connell.

Connell was so large and so close that Slocum might as well have had a wall between him and the new arrival. The big man took a quick glance over his shoulder and turned his attention back to Slocum.

"Don't test me!" the man behind Connell warned. "I swear I'll shoot you just to send a message to that red-haired little devil you work for. And believe me when I say I'd like to send a real nasty message to that one."

Connell must have believed him, because he unclasped his hands and stepped back.

"Now get out of here," the man behind Connell said.

When the big fellow started loping away, Slocum said, "I'm not about to let him just walk away! Not again!"

Since Connell was no longer taking up most of his field of vision, Slocum could see the squat figure who'd interrupted the brawl. He was obscured mostly by shadow, had a rifle to his shoulder, and was sighting along the top of its barrel.

"That devil I mentioned probably ain't far from here, mister," the shadowy man warned. "And there's a third man these two run with who could be watching from somewhere close right now. Are you ready to fight this big son of a bitch as well as two more that neither of us can even see?"

If he'd been holding a gun that was loaded, Slocum might have had a different answer to give. Instead, he spat out a curse and holstered his pistol.

"Whoever you are," Slocum said, "you'd better be real sure about letting this one go."

"I'm sure of one thing right now," the man replied. "We could both use a drink."

7

Rarely one to turn down a free drink, Slocum found himself at one of the smaller saloons on the corner of First Street and Dale Avenue. Named First and Dale, the saloon made up for its unimaginative title with a classically trained piano player and supposedly some of the best beer in Nevada. The music drifting through the air backed up the first claim, and Slocum waited impatiently at a round table for proof to verify the second.

The man who approached his table was barrel-chested and stout. He had the muscle and girth of someone a foot and a half taller who'd been squashed down to a more compact size. His head was bald and his eyebrows were bushy. Despite the roughness of his features, which gave him a naturally gruff appearance, he gripped a mug of beer in each hand and spoke in a subdued tone.

"I'm Scott Jeffries," he said while sitting down and placing the beers on the table. "I'm guessing you're John Slocum."

"You guessed right. I thought I was supposed to meet you at the One River."

"Part of the reason I wanted to have a word with you was because I've been tracking those robbers and heard you crossed paths with them. I spent the time before our appointment keeping an eye on that big son of a bitch. Soon as I saw him charge through the door of that cabin, I thought my assistance might be appreciated."

Slocum took a drink from his mug. It tasted all right, but he'd had plenty better. The brew's saving grace, however, was in its potency. That one sip was enough to tell him he could be drunk as a skunk in half the time if he didn't watch himself with the stuff. "How'd you know it was me when that big fellow and I came busting out of there?"

"The man at the hotel gave me a description. Also, that cut on your head is hard to miss."

"Which reminds me of another question. Why seek me out?"

Scott nodded and took a much larger drink of his beer than Slocum had. Judging by the stoic expression on his face, this wasn't the first time he'd experienced the potent mixture. "Since you were getting close to that woman, I thought you'd appreciate a warning about her. I saw your name on the hotel register. I heard a couple things about you."

"Like what?"

"Like you can handle yourself with a gun," Scott replied. "And that you've killed more than your share of men."

Although he was glad his mission with the Military Intelligence Corps was still mostly secret, Slocum wasn't exactly happy about what he'd heard. "If you're after a hired gun, I'm not the man you want."

"That's not what I'm after at all. I just thought you'd be interested in helping me track down the bunch that tried to rob you the last time you were in town."

"Tried?" Slocum scoffed before taking another drink. "Succeeded is more like it."

"Ain't nothing to be ashamed of," Scott told him. "Those robbers know what they're doing. They've had plenty of practice."

Slocum couldn't help noticing the venom dripping from Scott's words. "Why do I get the impression that you've got a personal stake in this? Something more than you just being on the receiving end of one of those bushwhackings."

"You'd be right about that, mister. I used to fancy myself a gambler. Did pretty good at the tables, too. When I met up with Heather, I thought I was lucky to get a wild, pretty little thing like that to take notice of me."

"Heather?" Slocum asked.

Scott nodded. "That's the name she was using before she started calling herself Kelly. I don't know for certain which of them is her real name or if either of them is."

"Go on."

"So when she first came around, Heather was as sweet as she could be. Made me feel real good . . . if you know what I mean."

"Oh, yeah," Slocum replied before taking another drink of his beer. "I know what you mean."

"We were together for some time when I noticed some of my money went missing. Not a lot, mind you, but enough to set me back a ways. I asked her about it and she 'fessed up to taking it." Shaking his head, Scott looked down into his beer and mused, "Funny thing is that I wasn't even really mad at her for it. I was just glad she'd told the truth so we could move along together." He glanced up as though he'd only just remembered that Slocum was sitting there. "I'd gone into a slump at the tables around that time, and when I started winning again, I thought maybe Heather was my lucky charm."

"I take it your luck ran out," Slocum said.

"Yep. Ran out all at once when two men jumped me and her in an alley after a four-day poker game in San Francisco. I'd won more than at any other game in my life. More than most of the other games put together actually."

"That's a hell of a good night," Slocum said. As much as he wanted to know exactly how much Scott had won, he decided not to indulge his curiosity by asking. He'd lost plenty of card games in his day and had been forced to part ways with large sums of money afterward. Telling the story to someone else only served to open old wounds for a fresh dose of salt. "Have I already made the acquaintance of those two men that robbed you?"

"You met one of them up close and personal tonight. That big bastard left welts on my head that I'll most likely take to my grave," Scott replied while reaching up to rub a spot that was located almost in the same location as where Slocum had been hit.

"Was the other one about my size?" Slocum asked, wishing he had more of a description to give. Fortunately, that seemed to be enough because Scott quickly nodded his head.

"Those two have been working together for some time as far as I can gather. That night in San Francisco when I was robbed, I found out the hard way that they had another partner." Scott took a pull from his beer that was big enough to earn Slocum's admiration. Setting the mug down without seeming to feel any ill effects from the powerful brew, Scott said, "I was about to go for my gun instead of handing my money over. Heather stopped me. I thought she was scared or maybe worried I might get hurt. She told me to do what they wanted. When I started to push her away so I could take care of business, I felt the knife in my back. Not like how folks say they got stabbed in the back. That woman put an honest-to-God knife in my back."

"Christ," Slocum grunted. "Did she stab you?"

"Not enough to kill me, but it caught my attention sure enough. When I felt the pain, I was more angry than anything else." Laughing without a lick of humor, Scott said, "I actually thought someone else had snuck past her to get to me. When I looked down to see that blade in her hand, I could hardly believe it."

"Sometimes it seems every woman is the devil's spawn."

"I don't know about the rest of 'em," Scott told him, "but that one sure is."

"That's why you're after her?" Slocum asked. "To pay her back for double-crossing you?"

"More or less. What she and them other two took from me that night was more than my dignity. The money I won was supposed to set me up in a better way of life. I was gonna open a business of my own. Maybe a saloon or a gambling hall where I could get a piece of every game instead of just my own. Maybe I could just open a store." He tightened his grip on his mug and stared down at it as if he were trying to boil his beer with nothing but bad intentions. "Or maybe I could just toss it into a river. The point is, it's mine and I ain't about to let her take it from me. After what she done to me and I don't even know how many other men, she don't deserve to just walk away."

"Well, we could have tracked them down a lot sooner if we didn't stop for drinks," Slocum pointed out.

Scott grinned widely to display a set of teeth that seemed as if they'd been sharpened by gnawing on gravel.

"She may have been running away when you last saw her, but the others in her gang were more than ready to watch her back."

"Did you see her running away?"

Flicking his eyes to meet Slocum's, Scott replied, "Yeah, I saw her. Naked as a jaybird and fast as greased lightning."

"About that . . ."

"If you're wondering how much I saw before she got away . . . it was enough for me to put together what the two of you were up to."

Slocum shifted in his chair. Although he didn't make a move for the gun he'd reloaded on his way to the saloon, he positioned himself so he could get to it as quickly as possible. "And that sets well with you?"

"After what I just told you, you think I may still be jealous that you took a tumble with Heather?"

All Slocum had to do was raise his eyebrows.

Scott rolled his eyes and said, "It stings, but that's what she does. You sure ain't the first man she's bedded since me. Besides, all she ever does it for is to get them to drop their guard or fall asleep or some other damn thing so she can steal from them and slip away afterward."

"Still doesn't make it any easier for you to sit across the table from one of those other men. And don't try to tell me you feel nothing for her anymore. I've played a few hands of poker myself and I can see that ain't true."

Scott held up both hands as if he were surrendering to a posse. "You might have a point, but I ain't in love. I just want to track her down and see that she don't hurt no one else."

"That's why you wanted to have a word with me?"

"Yep."

"How many others have you approached?"

"None," Scott replied. "Most of the men Heather sets her sights on are just idiots who do too much thinking with their peckers."

"Thanks a lot, friend."

"I didn't mean you." Scott laughed. "I meant those were the ones I didn't bother having a word with on account of them being too pissed off and crazy to be any use."

"But I'm different, huh?"

"Aren't you?"

Slocum wasn't sure how to answer that, so he shrugged it off and asked, "What do you need help with? You can't possibly think she's still got all of that money she took from you."

"No, but I know the three of them have pulled together a tidy little sum and they ain't keeping it in little towns like this one here."

Now Scott was moving into territory that interested Slocum the most. Wearing a straight face so as not to let Scott know just how interested he was, Slocum asked, "They take what they steal somewhere else?"

Scott nodded. "They go there once a place gets too hot for them to stay. Usually once someone finds out what kind of bitch Heather really is, the three of them ride away and lay low for a while until they find somewhere else to make a few dollars. After what's happened here tonight, I'd say they should be on their way real soon."

"Then we should hit them now!" Slocum said as he pushed away from the table and got to his feet. "We wait too long and they'll disappear."

Scott motioned for Slocum to sit down while taking a careful look around. The saloon wasn't very full, but some of the other drinkers in there were beginning to take notice of them. Once Slocum lowered himself back onto his chair, the locals got back to whatever it was they'd been doing.

"You don't think I already tried that?" Scott hissed. "When I first caught up to them after San Francisco, I rode straight at them. They scattered like goddamn dry leaves in a whirlwind. Knew exactly what they were doing and damn near killed me in the process. The instant I found some cover, they were gone."

"Then we'll just have to keep them fighting," Slocum offered. "Distract them from running long enough and one of us can—"

"No," Scott cut in. "They're too smart for that. Even if the first two get riled up enough to take the bait, Heather sure as hell won't. She'll go back to her hiding spot with a nice head start."

"And since you know where that is, we can catch up to her there."

Scott was shaking his head before Slocum had finished making his suggestion. "She's not stupid enough to just sit there and wait once she knows someone is nipping so close to her heels. She'll pull up stakes, find somewhere else to dig in, and hire on some new men to replace the ones she lost. That means tracking down which way she might have gone, finding out who Heather is passing herself off as this time, and scouting out who her new gunhands might be. If we let them get a head start now so they feel good and safe, we'll already know who we're dealing with."

Once Slocum got past the urge to chase after Kelly and her boys as quickly as possible, he could appreciate the reasoning behind Scott's words. The other man made a lot of sense, but there was still that burning ember inside Slocum's gut that made him want to ignore good sense and chase after her as quickly as his legs could carry him. No doubt, he wasn't the only man to have felt that same instinct. It was probably how Kelly had gotten as far as she had in her chosen life outside the law.

"God damn it," Slocum growled. "I should have just put her and that big bastard down when I had the chance."

"You thought you had a chance," Scott assured him, "but you didn't. The third one was out there, ready to pick you off if things got bad enough. He's the one in that gang that's racked up the most kills."

"So what are you proposing?" Slocum asked.

"What did she take from you? Whatever it was," Scott quickly added, "it must have been plenty valuable for you to come all the way back into town after leaving the way you did."

Slocum wasn't about to tell Scott about his business with Captain Vicker, so he kept quiet and let the other man talk.

"I can catch up to those thieves," Scott said. "When I do, I need help in bringing them down the right way. You help me with that, we get back what's ours. Simple as that."

Nothing was ever simple. Of the many lessons Slocum had been taught the hard way, that was a big one. Still, he believed that Scott could help him track Kelly and her two accomplices down. For the moment, there was only one question left.

"When do we leave?"

Scott smiled and replied, "Tomorrow morning. Soon as I toss a saddle onto my horse's back."

8

Before charging out to track down two slippery eels and one redheaded devil, Slocum retraced his steps from the last time he was in Pico Alto just to make sure he hadn't lost that page the old-fashioned way. After taking a look at the stable where he'd put his horse, the room where he'd stayed, and the Sunset Saloon, he was confident he hadn't dropped anything there. His next stop was the telegraph office, where he sent a message to Genoa for Tom. It read:

HAVENT FOUND ITEM **STOP** FOLLOWING LEAD
STOP MORE IN TWO DAYS **STOP SLOCUM**

Slocum figured that if he hadn't found the page by then, he would at least catch up to the robbers in that amount of time. When he thought about what he was chasing after, Slocum felt disgusted. There were a thousand things that could have happened to one damn piece of paper. For all he knew, the bundle had been short when it had been given to him. It wasn't as though he would have been able to make enough sense of the papers to know whether or not that was the case. As frustration started to build inside him, Slocum took a deep breath and pushed it back down again. All that was left now was to get some sleep and make certain he was at his best when it was time to leave. To that end, Slocum went back to his room, peeled off his shirt, and crawled into bed.

He wasn't sure exactly how long he'd been asleep when his eyes came open. The room was dark and the only sounds he heard were the ticking of the clock on the table beside his bed and footsteps creaking in the hallway outside his door. Slocum's eyes shifted in that direction to find the sliver of light between the door and frame to be just a little wider than he'd expected.

Slocum lay perfectly still and watched the door. After several seconds had passed, the door shifted slightly to make a grating creak of hinges in dire need of oil. When the door had been initially opened a crack, it must have made that same noise, which had woken him up in the first place. Watching as the door slowly came open, Slocum eased his hand beneath his blanket to get to the gun belt hanging from the bedpost. Just as his fingertips touched the brushed leather of his holster, the door opened wide enough to spill light from the hallway onto the Remington. Unsure as to whether or not his hand could be seen from the door, Slocum kept it right where it was.

The figure standing at the door was short and had long, thick hair. Once his eyes had adjusted to the difference in light at that part of the room, Slocum could make out a woman's curves beneath loosely fitted clothing. She eased the door open some more, took a cautious step inside, and waited.

Slocum watched her to see what she might do next. When he grew uncomfortable with waiting, he inched his hand once again toward his gun.

The woman at the door spotted the movement instantly and responded by turning her shoulder toward him and flicking one hand up and out.

It was too dark for Slocum to see the blade slicing through the air, but he could feel it well enough when it stuck between his fingers and pinned the holster to the post. A slow trickle of blood worked its way down Slocum's hand where the blade's edge had nicked him. Before the blood could roll all the way to his wrist, the woman had darted into his room and was crouched beside his bed.

"Where is it?" she asked in a harsh whisper.

"Who the hell are you?"

Slocum didn't see the second blade she carried until he felt the cold touch of sharpened steel against the side of his neck.

"The only question you need to ask," the woman said, "is how long you think you can last after I slice your throat open."

More than anything, Slocum wanted to push her back, grab that knife . . . do anything other than lay there. But whoever that woman was, she had him over a barrel. Her blade was already cutting into him, and any move he made would only hasten the process. As much as he hated to admit it, he had to play things her way for a while.

"Where is what?" he asked.

"The orders you're delivering for Captain Vicker. We know you have them."

"They're not with me."

As soon as those words left his mouth, Slocum felt the blade slide against his neck. "You think we're stupid?"

"I don't even know who . . . you are."

"We've been watching those Army men for months. Vicker and his spies have stayed put for a while and the only one who's come to see them is you."

"If you've been . . . watching so closely," Slocum said as best he could without moving more than a fraction of an inch in any direction, "you'd know that I already delivered what I was supposed to deliver."

"If you had, Vicker would have pulled up stakes and left by now. He hasn't, which means they're still waiting for something."

Suddenly, Slocum knew why sticking to the schedule had been so important to the Military Intelligence officer. "What makes . . . you think they're waiting . . . for me?"

"They only hired one civilian scout. One," she said while pressing the blade flat against his neck for emphasis. "That's you. Nobody else has spoken to any of those Army men."

"I . . . I don't know anything about that."

"Then why did you send them a telegram?"

Every one of Slocum's thoughts turned into a prolonged string of obscenities. Once that died down, he tried to think of just what the hell he'd gotten roped into. "T-Telegram?" he wheezed.

The blade pressed against his neck again. Slocum could tell it was being held at different angles, as though the woman holding it was already twisting it inside a wound. If she hadn't made such adjustments, the sharpened steel would have already sliced in too deep. After all, it wouldn't be wise to kill a man before he'd served his purpose.

"Don't treat me like a fool," she warned. "You sent a telegram this evening. What did it say?"

When Slocum spoke again, it was in a gasping croak. "You . . . were following me. Why . . . why don't you already know . . . what's in it?"

"Tell me or you die."

"I . . . can . . . can barely breathe."

The woman's face was so close to him and so obscured by shadows that Slocum could hardly make out any details. Her features were soft as a woman's, but also had the dreary quality of a painting that had been damaged by being left in a store window for too long. Her hair was the color of dirty straw, yet fine as cobwebs. For a moment, Slocum thought she would try to put an end to him right then and there. Slowly, reluctantly, she eased the blade back so he could fill his lungs without worrying about killing himself in the process.

That was exactly what he'd been trying to get her to do from the moment he'd started acting like a fish that had flopped out of water. As soon as he was given a bit of slack, he took full advantage of it by bringing his left hand up to grab hold of her wrist so she couldn't move the blade enough to do him in. He was at an awkward angle, but his right hand had a bit more room to maneuver. Instead of continuing to reach for the Remington, he grabbed as much of her hair as he could and pulled with everything he had. If he could have easily reached any other part of her with as much leverage as that, he would have. As it was, Slocum managed to pry the woman away from him before she could open his throat with the blade in her hand.

After she was forced away from the bed, the woman pulled her wrist free and regained her balance. Slocum balled his fist and cocked it back. The sight of the woman in front of him, even though she'd threatened his life seconds ago, made him pause before punching her in the face. She picked up on that right away and made it clear that she held no such reservations where his well-being was concerned.

She swung her blade at Slocum's face in a wide arc.

When he leaned back to clear a path for it, she drove one leg straight up between his legs. While Slocum may not have been ready to brawl with a woman, he was more than familiar with their preferred methods of fighting men. He was prepared for a blow below the belt and caught her leg in both hands.

"Ladies can never resist that target," he said. "Maybe that's how chivalry died."

Slocum held on for only a second or two until she attempted to get free by slicing at his fingers. Before the blade found him, he pushed her leg back in the hope of dropping her to the floor. The woman showed her impressive balance by hopping back until she could get both feet beneath her. All the while, she swung the knife wildly to keep him at bay. As soon as she reached the open door, the woman backed into the hall and slammed it shut behind her.

The first thing Slocum did was rush over to his bedpost and pull the knife from where it had been lodged, so he could retrieve his gun belt. After taking the Remington, he took a quick look at the cylinder to make sure it was loaded. There were bullets right where they should be, so he snapped the cylinder shut and cautiously approached the door.

Although he could hear a commotion in the hall, Slocum wasn't about to charge outside and into a possible ambush. When he reached the door, he stretched toward the handle and then pulled it open while hopping back a step. There was still a disturbance in the hallway, but it didn't look like the would-be assassin was in the thick of it. Instead, Slocum saw an older woman in a long cotton nightgown standing in the hall, shaking like a leaf.

"Did you see a woman with long hair pass through here?" he asked.

The old lady nodded, which set her silver-gray hair to swaying in all directions. Pointing a shriveled finger toward the door directly across from Slocum's, she said, "In there!"

Slocum immediately stepped into the hall and away from the door in case any shots were to be fired at him from the next room.

"I heard some sort of ruckus," the old woman declared. "When I opened my door to take a look, she came charging out of your room and straight into mine!"

Already inching toward the door to the old woman's room, Slocum tested the handle and found it was unlocked. Before opening it, he told the old lady, "Stand back. In fact, go downstairs to—"

"I'll get help!" she said in a rush.

Slocum was just happy that she hurried away and left him alone in the hall. He'd been listening for any movement from within the room and didn't hear anything. Without many options available, he took a deep breath and pushed the door open.

It moved less than a quarter of an inch before stopping dead.

"Shit," Slocum grunted. When he pushed on it harder, he could feel that something near the bottom of the door itself was wedging it in place. Since any element of surprise was already blown, he leaned his shoulder into it and knocked the door loose. The instant it swung open, he brought up the Remington and prepared to squeeze its trigger.

There was a lantern giving off a small amount of light in one corner, so he didn't need to adjust to total darkness. The room was similar to Slocum's in most respects: a scant amount of furnishings and one narrow bed. From where he stood, there wasn't much else to see apart from a window that had been flung wide open to let in a breeze, which brushed against a set of light yellow curtains.

Once again, Slocum fought back the urge to charge straight ahead. He dropped to one knee, lowering himself down to place a hand on the floor while simultaneously looking under the bed and aiming his gun in that direction. He found nothing but dust and the old lady's coin purse. Slocum finally charged toward the window and looked outside.

The instant he pulled the curtains aside, a small-caliber shot was fired up from the street. Recognizing the sound of a Derringer, Slocum wasn't overly concerned about being hit from that distance. He saw the short, long-haired assassin running across the lot behind the hotel, heading toward Second Street. Just below the window was a small ledge. Below that, a few crates were stacked up beside a side door that probably led into the hotel's kitchen. Slocum climbed out the window, placed both feet on the ledge, and hopped down onto the crates.

It wasn't much of a fall, but the crates had already absorbed one person's impact and started to give way from the second one's landing. As Slocum pushed off, he felt the crates teeter beneath him. By the time he reached the ground, they had fallen over amid a loud chorus of splintering wood.

The woman had disappeared into the shadows, and Slocum was cautious as he ran after her. He kept the Remington at hip level, ready to fire, while searching for any trace of his target. There wasn't much on that side of town apart from some houses and one or two shops that were closed for the night. As Slocum traversed a short alley to emerge from the other end, he saw more shops lining Second Street but nothing else.

Nobody was coming at him or running away.

There were no lanterns glowing in any windows.

When he saw something move from the corner of his eye, Slocum snapped his aim that way. A rat scurried from behind an empty water trough to make its way across the street, unaware that it had caught his eye.

Slocum wanted to keep looking for her, but his chances of finding anything useful had been whittled down to almost nothing. Second Street stretched in both directions right in front of him, dotted with darkened buildings and even darker alleys. There was also the possibility that the woman had circled around in any other direction, opening up the entire town for a search. Odds were good that she was watching him anyway and could either avoid him for as long as it took or attack him when the best opportunity presented itself.

If she was indeed watching, Slocum gave her something to see by spitting defiantly on the ground and walking back to the One River Hotel. There was definitely a fight coming, but he wasn't about to let it take place on her terms.

9

Slocum was still worked up from the excitement that night and wasn't able to get much more sleep. He was first to sit down to breakfast before the sun came up and was ready to leave when he was stopped by a tall fellow with a face full of stubble and a star pinned to his shirt. Several questions about the excitement from the night before were tossed at Slocum, which he answered as quickly as he could. The town's lawman was happy to get the answers and even happier when he decided that there wasn't much else to be done on the matter.

"Sounds like a woman who was touched in the head," the lawman said. "Wouldn't be the first one." Although he was chuckling, nobody else in the hotel's dining room enjoyed the joke. The old woman, who'd just come down for tea, sneered as if something sour had been squeezed into her cup. "Guess I'll be on my way," the lawman said. "I'd appreciate it if you stayed close in case I need you for anything else."

"Yeah," Slocum grunted.

With that, the lawman tipped his hat and left the hotel.

After settling his bill with the man behind the front desk, Slocum headed outside as well. The lawman had already made his way to a bakery that had just opened its doors for the day.

True to his word, Scott Jeffries was ready to ride as soon as Slocum found him at the stable. "Was that the sheriff coming out of the hotel?" Scott asked.

"Sure was," Slocum replied while climbing into his saddle.

Scott watched him for a second before asking, "What did he want?"

"How about I tell you while we ride?"

"Fine with me."

Scott led the way out of town and the two horses fell into an easy gallop that covered a good amount of ground without threatening to tire out the animals too early in the day. Once the trail stretched out before them and both riders could relax somewhat, Scott looked over to Slocum and asked, "So what did the sheriff want?"

Slocum gave him a short version of the story that included what had happened when he was attacked the night before. Some of the details he left out were the telegram he'd sent to Tom and the fact that the woman who'd broken into his room knew about it. When Slocum was through with his edited account of the events, Scott looked over at him with raised eyebrows.

"What?" Slocum asked. "Does that crazy woman sound familiar?"

"No. It just seems like you were supposed to have stayed in town."

"Why?"

"Because the sheriff told you to, that's why!"

"I don't owe a damn thing to that sheriff," Slocum said dismissively. "Or any other lawman, for that matter. Not until they earn my respect, and it takes a lot more than a piece of polished tin to cover any ground with me. I doubt that lazy fool will even realize I'm gone."

"Suppose it don't matter much anyway."

"That's right. So where are we headed?" Slocum asked.

Pointing a finger straight ahead, Scott replied, "North and then west. There's a little place just across the border in California called Saint's Row."

"Funny name for a place to find a gang of outlaws."

"Used to be a convent there, but there hasn't been a preacher in them walls for the better part of fourteen years. It's mostly a trading post now. You'll also find a few saloons and prospectors biding their time until they figure out which river they want to pan next."

"And Kelly or Heather or whatever the hell her name is . . . she's holed up there?" Slocum asked.

"That's where she and them friends of hers always go after things get too hot. After the lead they got on us, I reckon they'll be nice and comfortable by the time we catch up to them. Should make for a good surprise."

"A surprise, but not a fatal one."

Scott looked over to him. "Depends on how things go, I suppose."

"Seems like you don't want to kill her," Slocum said. "If you did, you should have been able to put a bullet into her by now."

"Maybe I just never got a clear shot."

Slocum chuckled and flicked his reins so his horse would keep pace with Scott's. "You expect me to believe that you followed them long enough to find as much as you did and you never got a chance to put her down like the mangy dog she is?"

Scott's reaction passed over his face like a moth flapping across a candle flame. When Slocum saw it, he snapped his fingers and said, "I knew it!"

"Knew what?" Scott grunted.

"You don't have any intention of harming a hair on that woman's head."

"I want to get what's mine. Ain't that what I told you? I already fessed up to how things were between me and her."

"How things were or how they are?"

"What the hell difference does it make?"

"Plenty," Slocum said. "If you're still sweet on this woman, that'll make a difference in how you act when we catch up to her. Maybe she gets the drop on us or pulls a gun. How can I be certain what side of the fence you'll end up on?"

"So what are you gettin' at, Slocum? You think I asked for your help so we could get close enough to Heather to give her a bunch of flowers?"

"I'm just trying to get a sense of what I'll be up against when the time comes. With you or without you, I'm tracking down that woman. If your intentions are what you say they are, then we'll wrap this up in no time at all. If you've got something else in mind, I'm not about to be shot or stabbed over it."

"Jesus Christ Almighty," Scott moaned. "If you were so squeamish about riding with me, you should've stayed in your damn hotel."

For the next couple of minutes, they rode in silence. Slocum kept his eyes pointed mostly forward, but was observing everything around him. He watched the trail ahead as well as the flat, barren land on either side for any hint of other riders trying to get close to them. Although the Nevada terrain was harsher than most, there weren't as many places to hide. He also got a feel for Scott's mannerisms. Everything from the way he sat in his saddle to how he held his reins was noted in Slocum's mind so he could watch for any changes when he asked his next couple of questions.

"Have you run afoul of any other women lately?"

Scott looked over at him, clearly taken aback by the inquiry. "I beg your pardon?"

"Maybe a short one with long brown hair and crazy eyes," Slocum replied. "The kind of woman that's got a penchant for knives."

"Are you serious?"

"Why wouldn't I be?"

"Because I don't know what the hell you're talking about right now."

"Sure you do. That crazy woman who attacked me," Slocum explained. "You changed the subject mighty quick when I brought her up last time."

"What more was there to say?"

"If she came after me, it's a fairly safe bet that she'll come after you sooner or later," Slocum said. He watched for a change in Scott's expression but didn't find one.

"I'll have to take my chances," Scott said.

"She's a killer. I could tell that much by looking in her eyes."

Still nothing from the other man, apart from a shrug and, "Then I'll be real careful."

At the very least, Slocum would have expected some hint of reservation from the other man. Only someone who'd already faced death at the hands of someone else could go up against a killer without pause. From everything he'd gathered so far, Slocum was certain that Scott wasn't that seasoned. That meant he must have known something on the subject at hand that allowed him to take some degree of comfort. Of course, there was also the possibility that Scott was so infatuated with his red-haired quarry that he was content just to be on his way to see her again.

Whichever of those two men Scott truly was, Slocum wasn't all that thrilled at the prospect of riding into gunfire with him.

10

The Alabaster in Reno, Nevada, was a tall, skinny building that stuck out among its neighbors. Somehow it looked as though it had been left to bake in the desert sun longer than any other nearby structure. Over the years, every plank in its exterior walls had been punished by heat, dust, wind, and all other manner of inclement weather. There was a bar on the bottom floor, but the place wasn't exactly a saloon. There were card tables on the first and second floors, but the Alabaster wasn't just a gambling hall either. A few beautiful women made themselves available to the gamblers, but nobody would mistake the place for a cathouse. The Alabaster was simply the Alabaster, and those who had business there usually had plenty of reasons to see it through without drawing attention to themselves.

As always, there were enough patrons scattered throughout the bottom floor to fill the air with a low hum of hushed voices. When the tall front door was opened so a petite woman could step inside, all the patrons looked in her direction. Once they saw that she was there on her own business with no indication that she would horn in on theirs, those people turned back around to continue whatever they'd been doing in the first place. In actuality, the only thing that could be called petite on the woman was her size. Although shorter than most, she carried herself with a man's confidence and kept her chin held high as if daring any of the men around her to give her the first bit of grief as she passed them by. None of them was stupid enough to accept that challenge.

By the time she got to the bar, there was already a small glass of gin waiting for her. She snatched it up, downed the liquor while walking, and slammed it onto the opposite end of the bar without breaking her stride. She then proceeded to the staircase that led to the next floor. Those stairs were too narrow for two people to pass going in opposite directions, no matter how small one of them was. Although the man who'd started climbing down them was much larger than the woman, he was quick to go back up and step aside so she could pass. She did so without a word of thanks, stomping toward the more intimate tables on that floor as if she would have plowed straight over him if the man had gotten in her way.

The only man in sight who didn't move was seated at a table near a tall rectangular window overlooking the street below. Even while reclining in his chair, he was a somewhat imposing figure. Long, thick legs, one crossed on top of the other, were encased in well-tailored silk pants. A matching suit jacket hung on the back of his chair, and a starched white shirt was buttoned all the way up to the string tie around his neck. A thick mane of dark hair was swept back to hang to his wide shoulders. He shifted in his seat, turning smoothly until he was facing the approaching woman.

"Back so soon?" he asked.

The woman didn't say a word. Instead, she reached out to grab his tie and pull it roughly. Even though she'd put some muscle behind it, her effort barely moved the man an inch. "It's not that far away," she said in a voice that reflected every bit of the ride that had brought her to that spot.

"What about your assignment?" the man asked. "I trust you were a bit more delicate in seeing it through."

Still maintaining her grip on his tie, the woman climbed onto his lap and sat astride him without seeming to notice how much she disrupted the table and everything on it along the way. When she pulled his tie again, she leaned her face in while bringing his slightly closer as well. "Nobody knew I was there," she whispered. "Not until it was too late."

"Unlike right now," the man replied in a vaguely scolding tone.

Easing back, she released his tie and shifted her hips. "Folks around here only care about what concerns them," she said while taking a slow look at the few others scattered among the nearby tables. "Anyone who was a threat to you wouldn't even be allowed up those stairs."

"There aren't many who pose a threat to me," the man replied as he took rough hold of the woman's hip.

She grinned. "I nearly killed that Slocum fella in Pico Alto," she whispered. "I could kill you, too, just as easily."

The man grinned also. One hand had been lying across his lap when she'd climbed aboard and had been partially trapped by her leg. Moving that hand slowly, he replied, "Could you?"

It was then that she felt the touch of iron against her thigh. The woman's eyes darted downward to verify that he was indeed holding a small revolver in his hand and was rubbing its barrel against the inside of her leg. "Yes, Duncan. I think I could," she said.

"Why don't you settle for telling me more about what happened in Pico Alto?"

"Not here."

"You already pointed out that this floor is a safe enough place to talk," Duncan replied. "As long as we keep our voices down."

"Maybe I don't like being so quiet."

Duncan's eyes narrowed as they locked on to hers. A few moments passed between them, each one sparking with tension that rippled through their bodies like hot fingers running beneath their clothes. A man in a dark blue suit entered the room after climbing the stairs from the first floor and made his way to a bulky figure seated at one of the other tables. Once there, the new arrival spoke to the seated man before turning around and heading straight back down the stairs from which he'd come.

Turning his attention back to the woman, Duncan said, "You never struck me as the subtle kind, Sarah. I'm still amazed by how well you perform your duties."

She climbed off him and gave his chest a little shove while swinging her leg over his lap. "I'll tell you all about it. What room are you in?"

"Twelve."

"Then get your ass in there," she said while turning toward the short hallway that led farther into the building. "I've got work to do."

Duncan took his time in getting to his feet. After placing the little revolver back into the holster tucked under his gun belt, he picked up his jacket and draped it over one arm. There were less than half a dozen others seated at various tables in the room, which was less than half the size of the room below it. Approaching the one who sat closest to the stairs, he patted him on a beefy shoulder and asked, "Can you keep an eye on things if I step out for a moment?"

"By the looks of that murderous filly," the bigger man replied, "you'll need more than a moment."

"Fine. Can you keep your eye on things for a *few* moments? Maybe a bit more if I decide to go in for thirds."

The man who was still seated wore a double rig holster around his waist. Compared to his bulk, the pistols kept there looked more like toys. The double-barreled shotgun propped against the leg of the table that was partially hidden by the tablecloth, on the other hand, looked very deadly indeed. He displayed the weapons and replied, "You're the one that hired me and the others, Duncan. You know damn well we can hold back anything short of a Gatling gun being fired through the windows. Anyone stomping up the stairs that we don't like will slide back to the ground floor in bloody chunks."

"That's what I like to hear." Duncan turned his gaze from the door that led to the staircase and toward a short row of rooms where the woman had disappeared. "Did you hear anything from Pico Alto?"

The big man with the shotgun shrugged. "You know Sarah better than I do. Ain't much to hear when she does a job. Usually, there's just a few bodies that need burying."

"What about the man she was sent after?"

"Name's John Slocum. Captain Vicker hired him to deliver them documents, which is exactly what he did."

"So the delivery has already been made?" Duncan asked.

"Something went wrong," the gunman replied. "Slocum was sent back to Pico Alto, wasn't he?"

"What about Vicker?"

"Him and the rest of those Military Intelligence boys are still in Genoa. The scout I sent couldn't get very close to any of 'em, but he knows for a fact they haven't left yet."

"What about the scout we sent to watch Pico Alto?"

"Nothing to report yet."

Duncan nodded slowly. "So either the delivery wasn't truly made or Vicker came up with another job that needed to be done."

Raising a quizzical eyebrow, the seated gunman asked, "Don't you think Sarah will have more to tell you than I do?"

"Most likely."

"Then . . . why are you still here with me?"

"Because, as with any other woman, it doesn't serve a man well to come the moment she beckons."

The gunman chuckled. "You wanna keep her waiting a spell, huh?"

"Precisely."

"Well, I wouldn't keep her waiting for too long," the gunman warned. "Sarah ain't exactly like any other woman."

"Which is why I've tolerated her for so long."

"As opposed to what?" the gunman asked with a laugh that shook his belly. "Cutting her loose? I wouldn't want to be the man given that job."

"You just worry about your job," Duncan said as he patted the other man on the shoulder. "I'll do mine."

"Some jobs are better than others, I imagine."

While loosening his tie so it could be removed from around his neck, Duncan replied, "Rank does have its privileges."

11

When Duncan opened the door to his rented room, Sarah was waiting impatiently for him. Her face was etched into a scowl and her hair hung around it like a wild mane. Although she had a penchant for dressing more like a man than a woman, she didn't look anything close to a man at the moment. The only stitch of clothing she wore was the shirt that had been on her throughout her entire ride. Its sleeves were rolled up past her elbows and it hung open to reveal a pair of ripe, firm tits. Kneeling on the bed, she straightened up so her shirt came open wide enough to display nipples that were only slightly darker than the rest of her skin.

"Where the hell have you been?" she asked petulantly.

Duncan pulled the door shut and placed his jacket upon a rack standing in the corner. "I should be the one asking questions. For instance, how did you get a key to my room?"

Smirking, she replied, "I don't need a key."

"That's right. You do have a knack for getting anywhere you want to go."

Peeling open her shirt even more, Sarah ran one hand past her breasts all the way down to the thatch of downy hair between her legs. "And I take what I want once I get there."

As much as he wanted to approach the bed, Duncan stayed put. His erection was already straining against his pants, and it grew harder as he watched Sarah slide her fingertips up and down along her pussy lips. It gave him some satisfaction to show her that she wasn't the one in charge. Turning his back on her, Duncan set about the tasks of opening a small valise and sifting through some random papers within. There wasn't much else in the room apart from the bed, a few small tables, and a writing desk, but he acted as though Sarah had already been forgotten.

"I can get the job done just fine without you," she warned.

When he heard the bed creak, Duncan glanced over there to find her sitting on the edge of the mattress with her legs spread. Both hands were between her thighs now and her eyes were partly shut in a drowsy expression as she put her fingers to work.

"Tell me what happened in Pico Alto," Duncan said. When he didn't get an immediate response, he turned around to find her staring back at him. Sarah's fingers were slowly moving between her legs, finding the exact spot where she wanted to keep them for a while.

"Answer me," he snapped.

"You always do this," she said. "Gotta remind everybody that you're the one giving orders."

Duncan approached the bed while unbuttoning his shirt. "I am the one in charge," he said sternly. "And don't you forget it."

Grinning as if she'd just accepted a challenge, Sarah eased the shirt off her shoulders so it hung off her bent arms. Her skin was smooth and her wild hair brushed against it invitingly as she lowered her head a bit to say, "Come a little closer and I'll pay the proper respect."

He stepped closer, but not until he'd unbuckled his gun belt and set it on the floor next to the desk.

As soon as he was in range, she reached out to grab hold of the front of his shirt and pulled him closer. Duncan allowed himself to be drawn in a step or two before taking hold of her wrist in a powerful grip and forcing her to let go. Sarah wilted, but only bent so she could reach behind her for a knife that had been on the bed. Since she'd been kneeling most of this time, the scabbard had been kept out of sight. She brought the blade up and snapped her hand around to deftly avoid it being trapped like her other one had been.

Despite feeling the touch of the blade against the side of his neck, Duncan remained poised. "Is that the knife you used on Slocum?" he asked.

"Yeah."

"But you didn't kill him."

"He didn't have anything to offer," she said.

"I suppose you questioned him?"

"I did," Sarah breathed. "Could have killed him if I'd wanted."

"Then why didn't you?"

"Because he had more to tell me."

"So," Duncan said carefully, "he got away from you."

"He put up a fight after he already proved that he didn't have much more to offer," Sarah replied plainly. "After that, it made more sense to get away before any law showed up . . . so that's what I did."

"Tell me everything that happened. Start to finish."

She smiled. "You gonna make me?" she challenged. "I'm the one with the blade to your throat. Doesn't that mean I'm the one with the upper hand?"

"It would," Duncan said, "if both of your hands weren't otherwise occupied." With that, he tightened his grip on her wrist while moving his empty hand down between her legs. The thatch of hair he found was already damp, and when he eased his fingers along the smooth skin of her wet lips, Sarah took a quick, excited breath.

The blade began to waver slightly against his skin. Duncan leaned in closer to smell Sarah's flesh as he slipped one finger and then another up into her. Slowly, her legs moved apart.

"You're not the only killer on the payroll, you know," he said. Before she could respond, Duncan reached inside her to find a spot that made her entire body tremble with pleasure. At the first hint of her eyes closing, he released the wrist he'd been gripping so he could snap that hand straight across and force the blade away from his throat.

Sarah chewed on her lower lip before saying, "You got the drop on me once. Now what?"

When he'd started this, Duncan's main concern was having a word with Sarah and getting her to tell him everything he needed to know. He'd worked with her plenty of times in the past, so he knew what she was like. He'd also bedded her several times in the past and knew that she enjoyed being able to hold that over his head almost as much as she seemed to enjoy the act itself. For that reason alone, Duncan had intended on steering her with a rigid hand until they arrived where he'd wanted them to go. Even though he knew to expect this sort of thing, there was only one rigid thing about him and it wasn't his hand.

"Now," he said. "You're going to do what I ask and tell me what Mr. Slocum had to say."

With a flick of her wrist, Sarah tossed her little blade aside. Before it had finished rattling against the floor, her hand was reaching between Duncan's legs.

He sneered as if he knew he was butting his head against a brick wall. The fact of the matter, of course, was that he simply couldn't hold himself back any longer. While Duncan may have released her as if he were letting go of a rotten slab of meat, he couldn't get his hands back on her quickly enough. He grabbed the edges of her shirt, used them to bring her in close, and then reached his hands beneath the weathered cotton.

"This what you want?" he grunted as he groped her plump backside.

Sarah was ripping his clothes off as best she could from her awkward angle. "You know it is," she said while pulling his shirt and tugging at his pants. When Duncan shoved her back again, she stared at him with wide eyes. He relished the fact that he could still surprise her every now and then.

By now, almost every article of Duncan's clothing was untucked, partially unbuttoned, or otherwise disheveled. He made quick work of getting out of his shirt and pants, freeing his erect member. As Sarah gazed hungrily at his cock, Duncan shoved her down and pulled her legs open wide.

"Did you fuck Slocum?" Duncan asked as he climbed onto the bed with her. "Is that why he's still alive?"

"No, sir," she said in a voice that was tense with excitement.

"Did you throw yourself at him?"

"No!"

Duncan positioned her so her legs were in the air and her ankles rested on his shoulders. Her pussy was wide open and his cock was aching to be inside her by the time he finally plunged it between her thighs. "You're not a killer," he said while pumping in and out. "You're just a whore."

Sarah smiled widely and leaned back as she groaned, "Only for you."

All of Duncan's previous plans went out the window as they so often did whenever he dealt with Sarah. She liked to think she had every man wrapped around her finger, but the reason why Duncan had survived her this long was that he kept her guessing on that account. The first time she'd thrown herself at him, Duncan was caught off his guard and happy to just enjoy the ride. As their work brought them together on other occasions, however, he realized he couldn't allow her to march in and get what she wanted. Soon he'd discovered that it felt good to take the reins from her. Damn good.

Sarah's legs were now pressed against his chest and shoulders as Duncan leaned down so he could clamp both hands over her breasts. He drove his thick shaft into her as deep as it would go, causing Sarah to arch her back and grip the blanket with both hands. Their eyes locked and neither one of them could make a sound apart from rhythmic grunting as their bodies collided. Her nipples became hard against his palms. Soon, however, she grew restless with her inability to do much of anything from her back.

When he felt her start to push him away, Duncan was inclined to stay where he was just to keep her from thinking she could tell him what to do. The muscles in her legs were too thick for him to resist very long. Also, he wanted to see what she had in mind. Smirking like a cat that had just trapped a rodent in a corner, she pulled herself up so she was kneeling on the bed.

"Get over here," she said with a slight growl.

Duncan did as he was told, but didn't lie down. Instead

of making her job any easier, he sat on the bed with one leg hanging over the side. Using the back of one hand, Sarah slapped Duncan's leg that was stretched on top of the mattress so she could crawl a bit closer to him. She then tugged his other leg to bring it back onto the bed. Now sitting between his legs, she faced him and reached down to start stroking his cock.

"Is this what you had in mind?" Duncan asked, trying not to react to the hand that was making him harder by the second. "We sit and stare into each other's eyes?"

Wincing as if the very notion of such intimacy was a disgusting joke, Sarah scooted forward and opened her legs so she could place her feet outside his hips. "No," she snapped. "This is what I had in mind." Now that she was sitting spread-eagle so close to him, Sarah could guide his rigid member back to the wet slit between her thighs. She leaned back once he was inside her, supported her weight using both hands behind her back, and started to grind her hips forward and back.

Duncan's attempt to remain aloof didn't last very long. Her pussy glided along his length even better than her hands had done a few moments ago. With just a little co-operation, he knew that pleasure would increase tenfold. Once he started pumping his hips in time with hers, he was proven wrong. It felt even better than he'd anticipated.

As he leaned back, Duncan felt his shoulders bump against the headboard. He pushed his feet into the mattress to gain some leverage so he could pound into her with more force. Sarah, however, had much more room to maneuver. She leaned back luxuriously, tossing her hair and moaning as she closed her eyes tightly. Her tits bounced every time his cock drove into her, and she moaned louder with every impact.

For the next several moments, they both forgot the roles

they'd been playing. Sarah was no longer acting the part of a wild horse and Duncan was no longer trying to tame her. He entered her and she took him in. When one of them started to move faster, the other kept pace.

Before long, Duncan was pounding into her with everything he had. Sarah opened her legs wider to accommodate him and leaned her head back until she was gazing up at the ceiling. Sweat rolled over their naked skin and muscles tensed as their bodies prepared for climax. It hit them at the same time, causing both to grunt loudly until it passed. When she was finally able to catch her breath, Sarah opened her eyes and looked at him once more.

"You haven't lost your touch," she said.

"Neither have you."

Her fingers were now drifting down between her thighs to brush against her clit and the cock that was still impaling her. "I could fuck you all night," she told him.

Duncan let out an exasperated breath, pulled out of her, and climbed off the bed.

"What's the matter?" she asked as she reached over for a nearby cloth to wipe away some of the slickness between her legs.

"You act like a whore," he replied.

"That's because you've never stopped treating me like one."

"And you say things just to get a rise out of me."

"If I get enough of a rise out of you, you'll treat me like a whore again," she told him with a smirk. "Now get back over here and taste what I've got for you."

"Tell me the rest of what happened in Pico Alto."

Sarah crawled on the bed so she was now the one with her back against the headboard. Even though she was still naked, she carried herself as if she'd encased herself in armor. "What more do you need to know?" she asked.

"Everything."

She rolled onto her side, reached down for her pile of clothes, and sifted through them until she found a pouch of tobacco, papers, and a box of matches. After sitting with her back straight and one leg stretched in front of her, she placed the paper just above her knee and opened her tobacco pouch. "Slocum sent a telegram to Genoa."

"And you're certain of that?"

Having poured out a narrow line of tobacco onto the paper, Sarah brought it to her mouth and ran the tip of her tongue along its edge. Watching him while knowing exactly what Duncan was thinking, she nodded.

Since he knew all too well the things of which her tongue was capable, he had a tough time maintaining his focus. "How did you come by this information?" he asked.

"I followed him, saw he went into the telegraph office."

"But how could you know where he sent his message?"

"Why the hell would I lie to you about that?" she snapped.

"Because you need to justify the ridiculous amount of money I pay for your services."

Spreading her legs just a bit wider, she said, "You seem to enjoy my services just fine."

Duncan had gone back to his clothes as well. Rather than pulling on his pants, he stooped down to pluck the .44 Colt from its holster. Although he didn't point the gun at her, he held it in a manner that would have made anyone nervous. "You'll answer my questions. There is a schedule to maintain and the information on those papers won't do us any good once that schedule runs its course."

Unlike most anyone else would have been in her position, Sarah wasn't nervous in the slightest. In fact, she took less notice of the gun in his hands than the one dangling between his legs. "The clerk at the telegraph office wasn't much more than a kid," she said while finishing up her cigarette. "I batted my eyelashes at him, put my hand on his pecker, and he told me where that telegram was going."

Resisting the urge to show his distaste for her methods, Duncan asked, "Did he tell you what was in Slocum's message?"

"He didn't remember that much."

"Or he wasn't about to tell you."

"No," she said. Now that the cigarette was between her lips, it bounced with every syllable. "He told me everything he knew. It just wasn't much."

"Perhaps he was stringing you along to get more out of you."

"No chance of that."

"Why?" Duncan sneered. "Because he couldn't possibly resist you when you were pleasuring him?"

"Oh, I wasn't pleasuring him for very long. After I gave him a few rubs, I went to work on his fingers." She struck a match against the bedpost and lit her cigarette. "Once I sliced one down to the bone, I just had to threaten to cut another one off and he told me everything."

Duncan appeared to be less disgusted by those details than the ones that had resulted in a smile on the young clerk's face. "What did the fellow have to say?"

"Just that the message Slocum sent was short and sweet. I think he was sent after the captain's papers sure enough, but he may or may not have them."

"May or may not? How does that help us?"

Sarah reclined against the headboard. "If he's got them, I can get them from him. If he doesn't, he knows where they are and will be going after them. Now that I know he still has business with those gents in Genoa, all I need to do is stay with him."

"Will you be able to find him?"

She nodded and blew a smoky breath toward the ceiling. "I can pick up his trail. That's the sort of thing you pay me for."

"Indeed it is." Despite whatever else Duncan may have thought of Sarah, he knew that she could do her job well enough. That was why she was still on his payroll instead of filling a shallow grave on a hillside somewhere.

"When I tore after Slocum, it lit a fire under his ass," she explained. "I couldn't just work on him like I did to that clerk. He requires a different sort of attention."

"But he got away," Duncan said. "In fact, I believe he nearly chased you down."

She shrugged and took another puff. "And now he'll be going to get them papers or whatever else Captain Vicker wanted him to get."

"What if he's already got what he needs and is getting away as we speak?"

When she smiled at him, it was obvious that Sarah had one more card to play. "What he needs," she told him, "was taken from him by some robber while he was in Pico Alto."

"And how do you know that?" Duncan asked.

"The soldier I bribed in Vicker's company found out about it and passed it along. Slocum must have gone back to Pico Alto to track the robber down, but that hardly matters because there's only one place where any robber is going to go in these parts when they want to disappear, and that's Saint's Row. It's not far from here."

Duncan scowled for a moment and then said, "I've never heard of it."

"That's the point. Not many folks have. Trust me, though, that's where this robber is headed, which means that's where Slocum is headed. All we'll need to do is post someone there and pick him off when he arrives. I can even keep Slocum busy enough that you should get a free shot at him."

After placing the gun down where it was out of her reach and still within his, Duncan lowered himself onto his knees beside the bed.

When he reached for her legs, Sarah asked, "What are you doing?"

"Rewarding you for a job well done," Duncan replied. He then proceeded to spread her legs and bury his face between them. First, he licked off a few spare flecks of tobacco that had fallen onto her thigh. Then he placed his mouth on her pussy and tasted her deeply.

Sarah leaned back, smoked her cigarette, and ran her fingers through his hair.

12

Slocum had never heard of Saint's Row. When he and Scott arrived there after a full day's ride, he got a real good idea of why that was. The place wasn't large enough to be considered a proper town. It was just a bit too large to be a camp. Some may have called it a settlement or possibly a village, but the term *row* suited it just fine. There was only one street lined with buildings meant to last for more than a week or two. Everything not facing that street was either a tent, a wagon, or an animal pen. Any other path branching off that street was hardly more than a set of ruts in the ground. What the place lacked in structures, however, it made up for in population.

"Where the hell do all these folks sleep?" Slocum wondered aloud as he rode down the street.

Scott rode beside him, watching as dozens of men with faces scorched by the sun and stained by the dust ambled back and forth in front of him. He shook his head slowly while replying, "I don't know. Looks like there's not enough town for so many people. Most of 'em don't exactly look like the settling kind, though. I'd wager they're just passing through."

That last part couldn't have been truer. Just looking around, Slocum thought he saw at least three or four men that were worth more dead than alive. Not exactly the kind of men who were wanted for well-known crimes, but petty thieves and those who'd run afoul of the law enough times to be pains in the asses of lawmen throughout California and its neighboring states.

Not all of those in sight were of the unsavory variety. Slocum also spotted a few men who swept the front porches of their businesses, keeping their heads down and trying to get along. Every town had men of this kind. They were the ones who put towns together in the first place. Without them, there would only be ramshackle camps that were too rowdy to keep from being burned down or knocked over. Tipping his hat to one such man in front of a feed store, Slocum said, "It won't be easy to find Kelly or her bushwhackers in this place."

"The phrase *needle in a haystack* comes to mind," Scott grunted.

"More like a particular needle in a stack of needles."

"Sounds about right. With either job, we stand to lose a fair amount of blood."

Slocum chuckled at that. Almost immediately, one of the nearby dregs heard the laugh and stopped in his tracks to face Slocum.

"Somethin' funny, asshole?" the tall man with a face full of greasy whiskers asked.

"We gotta start somewhere," Slocum said as he reined his horse to a stop. "Might as well be with this here fella."

"What did you have in mind?" Scott asked.

"Prob'ly wants to dance," the tall man in the street said

as he reached to his belt for the knife hanging there. When he drew the blade, he smiled as if he held the end of days in his hand. "Ain't that right, mister? You want to dance?"

Slocum dismounted and walked straight up to the man. It didn't take much to encourage him to swing the blade. All Slocum had to do was cock his head to one side and twitch forward as if he was about to lunge. The man bared his teeth and swung the knife at Slocum, only to be stopped by an arm that was brought up to halt the blade in the middle of its arc.

Keeping his left arm raised so he could prevent the knife from going any farther, Slocum snapped his right fist straight out to thump into the tall man's gut. After that, Slocum hit him in the same spot three additional times in rapid succession. By the time the punches stopped, the other man's eyes were wide as saucers and he gulped for breath like a salmon that had run afoul of a fishing hook.

A pair of somewhat smaller men stepped off the broken boardwalk with their hands resting upon their holsters. Spotting them immediately, Scott drew both of the .38-caliber revolvers slung under his arms and pointed one at each of the approaching men. "He a friend of yours?" Scott asked while nodding toward the big fellow with the knife.

Both other men nodded, albeit grudgingly.

"A good enough friend to throw yourselves in front of a bullet?"

One of the smaller men turned around and walked away without a second thought. The other shrugged and said, "Sorry, Bo," before following the first one's lead.

"Yeah, Bo," Slocum chuckled. "Sorry. Seems like you picked the wrong time to be such an asshole." He grabbed Bo's right wrist in both hands and then twisted. The smooth set of movements brought Bo to one knee while forcing him to release his grip on his knife. Slocum caught the knife by the handle less than an inch before it hit the ground.

"I ain't got nothin' worth stealing," Bo insisted.

"Funny you should mention that. My friend and I were looking for someone who's done some stealing."

"Toss a rock in any direction," Bo grunted as he reclaimed his aching right arm and held it close against his chest. "You're bound to hit a thief or some other no-good son of a bitch around here."

"Including you?"

The tall man didn't quite know what to say to that and tried to cover up that fact by gawking at Slocum with his mouth hanging open. Rather than watching that ugly display for another second, Slocum said, "I'm looking for someone in particular."

"Folks around here tend to look out for one another. You might want to watch your step around 'em."

"Watch our step, huh?" Scott asked. "So we don't upset any of these fine neighborly sorts who've been walking by for the last minute or two?"

At that moment, Slocum didn't know which was more amusing: the dozen or so men who went about their business without taking notice of the tall man being threatened at the end of a knife, or the shocked expression on Bo's face when he saw the same thing.

"I don't think anyone's coming to your rescue," Scott pointed out.

Placing the tip of the blade against Bo's stomach, Slocum said, "So much for honor among thieves."

"What makes you think I know who you're after anyway?" Bo grunted.

"She's fairly memorable, I reckon," Slocum replied.

"A she, huh? Plenty of them around here," Bo said while smirking up toward a trio of whores leaning out from a nearby second-floor window,

"Pretty face."

"That crosses most of these girls off the list," Scott said.

Bo looked over at him as if the two were old friends. "You got that right!"

"She's got red hair," Slocum continued. "And she's one hell of a thief."

"Ain't every woman?"

"This one's name is Kelly."

"Or Heather," Scott said.

Suddenly, Bo's eyes lit up like the Fourth of July. "Oh! You mean Cal?"

"Cal?"

Bo nodded and slapped Slocum's hand as if he was no longer afraid of the knife it wielded. "If you're after her, you won't be needing that. I'll tell you what you want."

Scott climbed down from his saddle. Since Bo no longer seemed to have much desire to fight and nobody around to back him up, Slocum tossed the knife he'd taken into the nearest water trough. He wasn't a fool, however, and kept his hand resting upon the grip of his holstered Remington.

"Why do you call her Cal?" Scott asked.

Bo dusted himself off as though his clothes were actually worth more than fourteen cents. "When she first came to town with them two partners of hers, she strutted around like the belle of the damn ball. Come to think of it, the dudes that accompanied her called her Heather but it wasn't long before she wrapped herself up and tried to pass herself off as a man. Called herself Cal after that."

"How do you know she and this Cal person are one and the same?" Scott asked.

"Ain't no man's got a figure as sweet as the one she's got," Bo replied. "Kind of hard to forget her. She's got red hair and robbed three men blind on her first day in town. I caught sight of her lifting the money from a man's pocket while he was scrapping with one of them partners of hers. She's got a real light touch and looks damn nice from behind. She's even got this tasty little freckle at the base of her neck—"

"Shut up," Scott growled as he balled both fists. To Slocum, he said, "This one's full of shit. He's just blowing smoke so we'll cut him loose."

"What did she do to you, Bo?" Slocum asked.

Confused by the stark contrast between the two men, Bo looked back and forth between Slocum's curious expression and Scott's intense glare.

"Go on and answer me," Slocum prodded.

Taking a step back to test that statement, Bo put some distance between himself and the other two. "I ain't no prisoner! Why would I help you?"

"Because there's obviously no love lost between you and Kelly . . . what did you say her last name was?"

Bo had to think about that for a few seconds and then shrugged. "I never did catch her last name. That ain't real unusual around Saint's Row. Most of us don't even give our real first names."

"Well, whatever she's calling herself," Slocum said, "we want to find her. It'd be in your best interest to help us."

"How do you figure?" Bo asked.

"Because it's the only chance you've got of getting back whatever she took from you."

Bo squinted. "How do you know she took anything from me?"

"That's what she does," Scott replied. "I doubt she's met anyone she didn't steal from."

"Three hundred dollars," Bo said. "That's what she took from me."

"Three hundred dollars?" Scott bellowed. "I bet you ain't ever seen that much—"

"We'll get it for you," Slocum cut in.

Studying Slocum carefully, Bo said, "Half up front."

"We haven't found it yet," Slocum replied. "How can I give you any of it?"

"What have you got?"

Slocum had to chuckle. Shaking his head, he patted his pockets while saying, "You've got some real sand, Bo."

"That's what I been told."

"A few seconds ago, I could have killed you. Now you're trying to wring cash from me?"

"Ain't nothin' is free," Bo said with a shrug.

"Why didn't you just ask for it in the first place?"

"Didn't know you wanted this little red-haired devil so badly. Seeing as how you do, you need to pay the piper. In case you haven't noticed, that'd be me."

"You're not the only one who can tell us what we want to know," Scott pointed out.

Bo nodded. "Sure, but that sweet little filly moves awfully quick. After this little ruckus we made out here on the street, she's bound to catch on that you two are in town and lookin' for her. Saint's Row ain't big and word spreads faster than greased shit over a frozen pond. You ain't got the time to go askin' around to anyone else. Even if you do find someone, she'll most likely be long gone."

"Why would you know where to find her anyway?" Scott asked.

Glancing over at Scott as though he'd already forgotten he was standing there, Bo replied, "Because I was plannin' on robbing her myself as soon as I got the chance."

"I've got twenty dollars," Slocum said as he pulled a few crumpled bills from his pocket. "Take it or leave it."

Bo snatched the money from his hand quick enough to make a man's eyes rattle. "I'll take it. She's stayin' at Mickey's. It's a hotel just down a ways. She's staying on the second floor."

"Which room?" Slocum asked.

"I don't know every damn thing!"

Slocum wasn't the trusting type on his best day and he'd learned to question the word of any man no matter who he was or what he was supposed to know. Dealing with the likes of Bo was never a matter of trust. It was in reading someone well enough to know when they'd been squeezed for every bit of usefulness they could offer. Whatever wellspring was inside Bo had just run dry.

"All right," Slocum said. "Where can we find you to bring you the rest of your money?"

Bo blinked several times before telling him, "Just go down to the Ocean Saloon and ask for me. They'll know where I am."

"Fine." When Bo didn't move, Slocum took a quick step toward him as if he was shooing away a yapping dog. "Go on, then!"

And just like that yapping dog, Bo turned tail to scamper away.

"There's a livery right over there," Slocum said as he pointed to the corral he'd just spotted. "Seems as good a place as any for our horses."

As they led their horses by the reins, Scott looked over his shoulder and grumbled, "That filthy idiot ain't never seen Kelly in his life."

"Sounds like he saw her to me."

"He just agreed to what you said so he could get some money offa you and you obliged!"

"At least now we've got somewhere to look," Slocum pointed out. "What would you rather do? Just keep riding up and down the streets of this filthy little place until we somehow stumble over the woman we're looking for?"

"It'd be better than taking the word of some piece of gutter trash." After taking a moment to consider that, Scott added, "Perhaps not, but I still don't trust that fella."

"I don't trust him either," Slocum said. "But I do think Kelly has taken something from him. At the very least, she piques Bo's interest enough for him to want her found. Most likely, he knows she's holding on to someone's money and he thinks he can turn a profit by staking a claim on however much is in her pockets."

"Knowing the sorts of things that she's been up to," Scott grunted, "there's bound to be a price on her head. Could be he wants to cash in on that once we do the dirty work of clearing out her partners."

"Now you're talking!"

Scott looked over at Slocum, and for the first time in a while, he didn't seem ready to spit. "What are you so happy about?"

"We're making progress," Slocum replied.

Now Scott let out a genuine belly laugh. "Progress? You should save a word like that until we actually catch sight of her. I still say that asshole back there ain't never even laid eyes on Kelly."

"Oh, he's seen her all right."

"What makes you so sure of that?" Scott asked.

"Because he was right about one thing at least. She does have a tasty little freckle at the base of her neck."

Scott gripped his reins a little tighter. If there was any doubt in Slocum's mind about feelings that might have remained in the other man's head where Kelly was concerned, they were wiped away now. Just to be on the safe side, Slocum walked on the other side of his horse so he was out of Scott's reach.

13

After putting their horses up at the stable Slocum had found, he and Scott walked to Mickey's Inn. It wasn't difficult to figure out which way to go. The man at the stable pointed them in the right direction while giving them a few simple instructions.

"Can't miss it," the stableman had said. "Place was just opened a month ago. Best card games in town."

The description had seemed cryptic, but the stench of whiskey on the stableman's breath was strong enough to convince Slocum that there wouldn't be much else of use coming out of him until he sobered up. Not wanting to wait that long, both Slocum and Scott had tipped their hats and went on their way. After a small walk in the direction they'd been steered, Slocum said, "I'd imagine that's the place."

"Me, too," Scott replied. "Guess it truly is hard to miss."

Since it was the only building that didn't look as if it had been set on fire in the last few weeks, Mickey's stuck out like a single clean tooth in a putrid mouth. Rather than walking straight up to the place, Slocum and Scott stepped onto the boardwalk across from it and made a slower approach. Once they had the hotel squarely in their sights, they stopped and leaned against a post as if they were just another pair of friends shooting the breeze.

"How should we do this?" Scott asked.

"I figure one of us heads up to the third floor and the other watches his back. Since it was my idea to ask for advice from a mangy dog like Bo, I reckon I'll be the one to take the lead. All right, then," Slocum sighed. "Here I go."

He was stopped before taking his first step when Scott reached out to slap the back of his hand against Slocum's chest. "I'll go in first," Scott said. "Give me a minute or so to get situated at the bar or find a seat where I can watch the door. It wouldn't look anything but suspicious if we both marched in there like a posse."

"Good point," Slocum conceded. "After you."

Scott slid his hat forward so its brim covered a good portion of his face. He crossed the street, stomping through a few deep puddles marring the crooked and poorly maintained path through the middle of Saint's Row. There was a steady stream of dirty men moving up and down the street like muddy water in a gurgling creek. None of them glanced at anyone else for more than the time it took to look away again. Even so, Slocum was fairly certain most of them were seeing plenty. No outlaw worth his salt could live for more than a week without being wary of his surroundings.

He watched Scott navigate through the flow of horses and burly men walking with their heads hanging low. When Scott reached Mickey's front door, he pulled it open and was immediately met by a bear of a man who was wide enough to act as another door entirely. Even though he couldn't hear what the two of them were saying when they exchanged words, Slocum reflexively placed his hand on top of his holstered .45.

"Come on," Slocum said under his breath. "Don't push too hard. Just make up a simple lie and move along."

Whatever Scott was saying, the big man guarding the door wasn't liking it. When Scott attempted to step inside the place, the big man roughly pushed him back outside with one paw of a hand.

"God damn it," Slocum said. "Don't be stupid. Just get inside. Pay him if you have to, for Christ's sake. How hard is that to figure out?"

As if hearing Slocum's snarling words or picking up on the thoughts racing through his head, Scott placated the big doorman with a clumsy smirk and a few words. Slowly, Scott reached for a pocket and removed something that glinted in the light. When Slocum spotted the silver dollar, he grinned. "That's the way. Nice and easy."

The coin was enveloped in the big doorman's hand and wasn't to be seen again. Finally, he stepped aside and allowed Scott to enter. After glancing to either side to make sure nobody else wanted to get past him, the big fellow closed the front door.

Slocum kept his hand on his Remington, but wasn't tensed for a quick draw. Instead, he leaned against the post outside a store with a front window that was so dirty he couldn't make out one letter painted upon the glass. It didn't matter what was sold inside that store or whether it was a store at all. All Slocum needed was a place to stand for a few more minutes, which was exactly what he got.

Better than any watch, Slocum's gut told him when it was time to step away from the spot he'd been haunting. The instant he peeled his shoulder from the post, he heard a harsh whisper come from directly behind him.

"Stay still," it said.

When Slocum started to turn around, he felt something jab into the small of his back.

"That was the exact opposite of standing still," the voice reminded him.

Although the voice was too scratchy and strained for him to make out very much, Slocum could definitely tell that it came from a female. "Do I know you?" he asked. "You sound familiar, but then again I've heard plenty of women's voices in my day."

"Oh, have you now?"

That comment would have gotten a rise out of just about any woman and this one was no exception. Now that he could hear more of an actual voice instead of a grating whisper, he was able to pick out some finer details. The woman leaned in closer and spoke so he could feel her warm breath on his ear. "And just how many others have there been since we shared a bed, John?"

"Kelly? What the hell are you doing?"

"Judging by the surprise I hear, I'm guessing there's been at least one woman since me. You're a swift mover."

At first, he thought it was a blade being jabbed into his back. Now that he knew who he was dealing with, he had a much better idea of the sort of weapon she preferred. He hadn't heard a hammer snap back, which meant she wasn't quite ready to burn him down. She could very well have cocked the little gun beforehand, but Slocum was prepared to make that gamble.

Pivoting around, he brushed away her weapon with his body and followed through with his closest hand. Sure enough, it was a two-shot pistol gripped tightly in Kelly's hand. She'd allowed him to turn partway around, but wasn't about to let him take the gun away from her.

"You seem surprised to see me," she said. "And here I thought you were tracking me down."

"I am. We have some unfinished business to tend to."

She licked her bottom lip and let her gaze snap down below Slocum's belt for an instant. "I know. I've been thinking about that for a while."

"You took something of mine," Slocum said.

"You got your watch back. Did it belong to your pappy or something?"

"I'm not talking about the watch. You know goddamn well what I'm after."

"I don't," she said.

"Your partners are in there, right?" Slocum said as he hooked a finger toward Mickey's.

Pressing the gun into Slocum's ribs, she stood her ground and said, "One of them is. The other is watching me right now."

"I don't care about that." When he tried to get even closer to her, Slocum felt the pistol dig into him a bit more. The gun may have been small, but it was still enough to put him in a world of pain at such close range. "I did come a long way to find you," he said. "That doesn't mean it has to be unpleasant."

"And what were you going to do when you found me? Sweep me away to some dance hall?"

"If our business concluded well enough . . . perhaps."

"Please," she scoffed. "I've had plenty of other men try to sweet-talk me and they did a much better job."

"Okay," Slocum said. "You got the drop on me. Now what?"

"I was about to ask you the same thing."

"You're the one in control here, red."

Kelly grimaced. "Don't treat me like an idiot. You're the one trying to lure me to that hotel. What's waiting inside for me? A posse? No," she said quickly. "A posse wouldn't last long in this town."

"Wait," Slocum said. "You're supposed to be the one in there. If anything, I figured I was the one being steered to this spot."

"Steered by who?"

"You know a man named Bo? Filthy-looking fellow. Dumber than a sack of rocks."

"You'll have to narrow it down a bit more than that," she said.

"He told me you stole from him."

Drawing a breath that was surely meant to tell Slocum he still wasn't any closer with his description, Kelly paused and squinted at him. "Was he that man you were talking to on the street not too long ago?"

"Yes. How long were you watching me?"

"Since the moment you rode into town," she replied proudly.

Saint's Row wasn't a quiet place. Ever since Slocum had arrived, the air had been filled with bawdy laughter, raucous music, women's screams, shouted obscenities, and every other manner of noise that could reflect anything from fear to ecstasy. Gunshots were occasionally tossed into the mix, but were usually muffled or in the distance. This time, they were much closer. Close enough to draw both Slocum's and Kelly's attention.

"Whatever trap you set up," she said, "it sounds like it's been sprung."

"I didn't set any trap. I barely knew where to start looking for you."

Normally, Slocum wouldn't tip his hand that way. Even under the best circumstances, an act like that couldn't lead to good things. This time, however, he needed to make a quick decision and spark a reaction to help him figure out which choice to make. He got what he was after when he saw the confusion on Kelly's face, followed by growing concern as she looked toward Mickey's.

"What's happening in there, John?" she asked. "It sounds bad."

There was more shooting as well as the pounding of hurried footsteps from within the place across the street. "Should we look into it for ourselves?" he asked. "Or do you still want to shoot me?"

Kelly glanced down and seemed surprised to find the pistol in her hand. Quickly, she eased the weapon away from Slocum's ribs and lowered it. "If this is another trick," she warned, "I can shoot you just as easily as before."

"Yeah," Slocum replied as he turned to face Mickey's. "I believe it."

Just then, the hotel's front door was thrown open and a short stream of well-dressed men hurried outside. A few women in expensive dresses followed them, and two more men brought up the rear. The big guard was one of those and Scott was the other.

Since Kelly was taking in the sights just as well as he was, Slocum prepared to draw his Remington when he said, "There you go. That's another man who'd like to have a word with you about a few things. I'm sure you know him."

"No," she said. "I've never seen him before."

What troubled Slocum the most was that he believed her.

14

There had been no change in her face.

No twitch when she saw Scott rush out of Mickey's.

No hint of recognition when Scott looked across the street for Slocum.

Not even a twinge of anxiousness upon setting eyes on one of the many men she'd wronged. Even for the most experienced outlaw, that last one was a tough thing to mask.

"That's Scott Jeffries," Slocum said.

Still nothing came from her, other than a grunted, "Who?"

That's when Slocum did see something that gave him some insight into another person's intentions. Unfortunately, that other person wasn't Kelly. It was Scott and his entire face darkened once he got a look at the two people standing across the street. Without hesitation, Scott brought up the gun in his hand and fired.

"Jesus!" Kelly shouted as she leapt to one side so she

could get behind the post next to Slocum's. "Who the hell is that?"

"You truly don't know?"

"No!"

They were interrupted by another gunshot. This one blasted through the air to knock a chunk out of the post inches away from Slocum's face. Leaning from his slender bit of cover, Slocum shouted, "It's me, you damn fool!"

Scott had stepped down into the street by now and was firing again. One shot was for Kelly and another chipped away at the post closest to Slocum.

"I don't think he much cares for either of us," she said.

Slocum couldn't argue with that, and he sure as hell wasn't about to stay put until he was gunned down for no good reason. Drawing the Remington from his holster, he moved away from the post and pivoted into a sideways stance so Scott had less of a target. Now that he had a few seconds to take aim, Scott sighted along the top of his pistol and squeezed off a careful shot. The only reason it didn't burn through Slocum's back or any other piece of him that couldn't be concealed by the post was because Slocum had seen where the gun was being pointed and made a last-second dive to a different spot.

The door to the dirty little storefront behind Slocum had been partially open the entire time. It may have been impossible to read the lettering on the filthy window, but he didn't need to know what those words said before ducking into the store and putting his back against the wall beside the door.

"What's happening here, John?" Kelly asked from outside.

Another shot was fired before Slocum replied, "I'm still trying to figure that out." He raised his voice to holler,

"Maybe you can help me here, Scott! What the hell is going on?"

"You know damn well what's happening, you traitorous son of a bitch!" Scott shouted back. "Now that you met up with Heather behind my back, come on out here and get what's coming to you!"

"John," Kelly said in a voice that was just loud enough to reach Slocum's ears. "I think we should both get away from here."

"Yeah," Slocum replied. "I think you're right."

Kelly looked back at Slocum, but seemed reluctant to make another move. That hesitation wasn't unfounded since Slocum was still holding his Remington at the ready, but it left her as soon as Scott fired another shot. When she ran from her post, more shots exploded behind her as several of the other gunmen in the street opened fire.

Slocum held the door open until Kelly had bolted past him and into the store. He then kicked it shut and followed her down an aisle between two tall sets of shelves that held nothing but dust and cracked mason jars. A volley of gunfire chopped through the door and knocked out portions of the window, allowing a trickle of light from the outside world to make it into the musty space.

All that concerned him was a door at the farthest end of the room being opened by a short man dressed in a simple white shirt and what looked to be an old blacksmith's apron. Smoke billowed from the room behind him and the air suddenly reeked of fire and ash. "You better have a good reason for bustin' in here!" he shouted. He raised the hand that had been partially hidden behind his apron to reveal a sawed-off shotgun. "If you think you're robbing me, then you got a fight on yer hands!"

Slocum and Kelly were still moving. She barely took

the time to look in the direction of the man in the apron, but Slocum glanced over there to catch sight of the room the man had come from. He could see a small pile of plates, silverware, and some other odds and ends that looked to have been collected from a multitude of homes. Something was spewing steam from the back of that room and he doubted it was a fireplace.

"We're just passing through," Slocum said to the man, who'd planted his feet to guard the doorway. "Is there another way out of here?"

"Go back out the way you came, damn it!" the blacksmith said.

"John! I found a back door," Kelly shouted. "Hurry!" She was moving like her tail had been set on fire and barely slowed down to open the door she'd found instead of stampeding straight through it.

Slocum tapped the brim of his hat in a quick salute while saying, "We'll be on our way. Thanks."

"Thanks my ass!" the blacksmith snarled. "Just who the hell—"

He was cut short by the smashing of the front door as Scott kicked it in. The blacksmith snarled something, but his voice was eclipsed by the roar of his shotgun.

Slocum caught a glimpse of what was happening just before he followed Kelly out of the shop. Scott dove to one side as buckshot ripped into the front door's frame and window. Rotten splinters of wood and chunks of dirty glass filled the air as the shotgun did its work. Rather than sticking around to see what happened next, Slocum quickened his pace to catch up to Kelly.

She must have heard the steps drawing closer to her back because Kelly took a quick look over her shoulder while continuing to run. "What was that?" she asked breathlessly.

"Looks like a smelting shop," Slocum replied. "Probably

melting down stolen gold and silver so it can't be linked back to where it came from."

"As long as they're kept busy, I don't care what that blacksmith is doing. There's more of those gunmen coming," she said. "Sounds like from that way."

They were in a narrow lot behind the old shop. When Slocum looked in the direction she was pointing, he found a narrow alley between the shop and its neighbor as well as an outhouse that looked to be one stiff breeze away from collapsing into a pile of sawdust. His ears were still ringing from the shotgun blast, but Slocum decided to take Kelly at her word.

As soon as she reached the edge of the lot, Kelly stopped. Rather than jumping over the broken fence marking the edge of the smith's property, she put her back to the warped wooden beam and stood with her back straight.

"What the hell are you doing?" Slocum asked as he thundered toward her.

"Presenting a nice target."

"You're crazy, god damn it," he grunted as he lowered his shoulder and charged at her like a bull.

Kelly's eyes widened in surprise when it became obvious that Slocum had no intention of stopping. She braced herself, held out both arms, and said, "Now wait a sec—" before he plowed into her midsection.

Upon making contact with her, Slocum wrapped one arm around Kelly's slender waist and slapped the other hand on top of the fence. From there, he let his momentum carry them both over the fence to land in a heap on the other side. It wasn't pretty, but he wound up on top of her in a pile of tall weeds.

A shot cracked through the air and Slocum smirked.

"See that?" he said. "I was just in time."

"Just in time for what?" she grunted while struggling

to get out from under his weight. "To break every last one of my damn ribs?"

Rolling to one side while repositioning himself to get a look at the mess behind them, he said, "A thank-you might be in order. You know . . . for putting you out of the way of a bullet and all."

"You're sure about that?"

A man stood at the back door of the shop. He wasn't the stout fellow in the blacksmith's apron, but a taller man holding a pistol in his hand. A bloodstain was forming on his left side. He looked up and then down before spotting Slocum and Kelly just beyond the fence. He'd barely raised his pistol to take aim when another shot was fired. It sounded similar to the first and the bullet that was fired caught the gunman squarely in the chest. The man fell back and hit the floor with a heavy thump.

Too pleased with herself to contain it, Kelly beamed with a smug grin and said, "See? I told you my other partner was watching out for me."

"That was one of yours?"

She nodded. "Brackett's one hell of a shot. Even when he's drunk."

Before the first gunman had a chance to spit out his last breath, another hurried out of the shop. He was stopped by a rifle shot that knocked a hole into the wall a few inches from his head. When he backed up, he slammed into Scott, who'd been hot on his heels.

"Get movin', damn you!" Scott roared.

"There's a man with a rifle out there!" the gunman replied. "He already got Mark!"

Scott took a quick look down, saw the man who'd been shot, and looked up again. By then, Slocum and Kelly were on their feet and heading through the weeds beyond the fence. Scott brought up one of his .38s and sent a few rounds toward them.

Placing a hand on Kelly's back, Slocum shoved her down while hurrying her along. "Watch yourself or you'll catch a piece of lead!" he warned her.

"Brackett ain't about to let them pass."

When the next rifle shot was fired, Slocum was able to trace the sound back to its origin. He eventually spotted the silhouette of the third bushwhacker from Pico Alto. Brackett stood on the roof of a house that was just tall enough to get a good view of the street as well as Mickey's. Now that they'd emerged from the back end of the old shop, Slocum and Kelly were in the marksman's sights as well. She looked up at the roof and tossed a wave at Brackett. The rifleman nodded once and quickly brought his weapon up to his shoulder.

"There he is!" Scott shouted.

Those words were barely out of his mouth when a volley of gunshots erupted from behind the smith's store. Screaming, Kelly took aim with her pistol and fired both of its shots toward the gunmen. The little pistol may have been effective up close, but it was good for nothing at a distance.

Grabbing her arm, Slocum said, "Come on!"

But Kelly wouldn't move from her spot until she got another look at the rooftop where Brackett had been perched. The rifleman was firing as rapidly as he could lever fresh rounds into place and even managed to put down the gunman beside Scott like he was a tin can being knocked off a post. None of that was enough, however, to keep him alive for long.

Slocum saw a spray of blood when Brackett had caught a round and he saw another when Scott's .38 punched a hole through his chest. The rifleman slumped, fell backward, and dropped out of sight.

"That's it, we gotta go," Slocum insisted.

Kelly was moving, but not very quickly. "But there's only one of them left," she said.

"Only one that we can see," Slocum told her. "I can hear plenty more."

She was about to protest, but the voices echoing from one of the nearby alleys made it tough for her to argue against Slocum's point. Not only was it impossible to tell the exact spot those voices were coming from, but they were getting louder with each passing second. Finally, she closed her mouth into a determined line and turned her back on the shop.

More than happy to follow her, Slocum fired a pair of rounds at the shop. Without knowing how many others he was up against, he wasn't about to stand his ground so anyone else could find a good vantage point and pick him off. Instead, he settled for sending a few deadly regards sailing in Scott's direction. One of them punched into the back wall of the shop and the other must have gotten real close to its mark because Scott jumped out of the doorway in a rush.

It took some work, but Slocum managed to catch up to Kelly. Without breaking stride, she made a sharp left and ran toward the back of a building that was twice as wide and half as dirty as the shop they'd left behind. "Who are those men?" she asked.

"I only know one of them," Slocum replied. "Or I thought I did."

"Did you know he meant to shoot us?"

"Not exactly."

Having reached the wide building, Kelly slowed her pace and tucked the pistol into a pocket of her jeans. She was dressed like a cowboy that had just climbed down from the back of a horse and still somehow managed to look appealing. Combing her fingers through her hair to tousle it even further, she said, "Then I'd say you don't know him at all. Don't feel bad. You're not the first to be tricked by a lying asshole."

She reached out for the handle of a door at the top of two steps leading up from the uneven ground. Slocum took a quick look around as more gunshots echoed in the distance. Since they weren't coming from the direction of the blacksmith's shop, he figured they were connected to a different argument altogether. Just another happy day in Saint's Row.

The door came open with little convincing required. Kelly tossed her hair back and strutted inside as if the deed to the place were in her hip pocket. After a few more steps, a man about her height and nearly double her width blocked her way.

"Clear a path . . . oh," the fat man said, obviously taken aback by the pretty woman wrapped up in a man's clothes. "Sorry, ma'am. Go right on ahead."

She smiled and reached out to brush her fingertips along the rippling layers of the man's chins. "Much obliged, stud. Think you can do me a favor?"

Slocum holstered his Remington, but kept his hand on its grip as he cracked open the door they'd just used so he could take a quick gander outside. So far, all he could see was the back side of the main street and a long row of outhouses, but he knew that area could be getting more crowded in no time at all.

Not concerned with anything other than the soft touch of a woman against his face, the fat man nodded. "Sure I can do you a favor. What've you got in mind?"

"Could be some men asking about me," she said.

"Lawmen. They think I stole something from a lying piece of shit in Fresno."

The fat man's blubbery face shifted into something close to a smile. "You say they's lawmen?"

"That's what I said," she told him with a nod.

Looking over to Slocum, the fat man asked, "Lawmen in Saint's Row? You sure about that?"

Slocum followed her lead by saying, "Either lawmen or bounty hunters."

Judging by the look on the fat man's face, he despised both of those options equally. "I'm on my way out to the shit house," he grunted. Looking back to Kelly, he asked, "If'n I do discourage them lawmen from coming round here, you'll owe me."

She pressed herself against him and placed her face so close to his that her lips brushed against the fat man's cheek when she said, "You bet your ass I'll owe you."

When the fat man started moving again, there was a purpose behind his strides. Slocum stepped aside and put his back to the wall as the fat man opened the door and waddled through. Almost immediately, several voices drifted in from the outside.

"You seen a woman come this way?" someone asked. Slocum looked through the crack in the door, but couldn't see much. He didn't want to open it any farther since the movement would draw unwanted attention straight to him.

"You want a woman?" the fat man grunted. "Go in and buy one like everyone else."

"I ain't talking about no whore. She's a thief. Red hair. Skinny. Dressed like a—"

"Shut yer goddamn mouth, law dog!" the fat man grunted.

Knowing things would only get worse from there, Slocum eased the door shut and walked quickly down the short hallway to catch up to Kelly.

"Come on," she said without needing to look back to see who was behind her. "Let's get a drink."

The sounds and smells coming from the next room told Slocum that the place was a saloon. As much as he wanted to keep moving, he stayed with Kelly for the moment. She seemed to know what she was doing well enough.

15

The place was a saloon, all right. Slocum didn't know the name of it, but it was full to brimming with rowdy people and whiskey. That was all he needed to know. As for Kelly, she wound through the milling crowd and got all the way to the bar, where she somehow walked away with two drinks without paying for them. Slocum picked a spot that was close to the wall with a good view of the front and back doors.

When she made her way to the table, Slocum lowered himself onto a rickety chair. "You got a lot of friends here?" he asked as soon as Kelly was close enough to hear him over the noise filling the air.

"Nobody has many friends in this town," she replied. The smile she'd worn left her face the moment she set the two glasses onto the table and sat down.

"Then what makes you think you're safe in here?"

"Because it's full of people and none of them will be frightened by someone charging in here with a gun."

"I take it you're doing more than just guessing in that regard?"

"Of course I'm not guessing," she snapped. "I scout for places like this the moment I ride into a town. The nice thing about Saint's Row is that just about every place is like this one."

There was a commotion toward the back of the large room. Slocum looked past the bar, past the poker games going on at other tables, and past the soiled doves plying their trade in varying degrees of undress. Even with so many distractions, he was able to spot a few angry faces emerging from the hallway that led to the back door he and Kelly had used to get into the saloon. Before long, those angry faces were surrounded by some even angrier ones.

"Looks like your fat suitor didn't do a very good job of steering them away from here," Slocum pointed out.

"Just stay where you are and act like you belong here."

"How do you propose I do that?"

She answered him by pulling her shirt mostly open and mounting his lap. A few of the nearby drinkers laughed at her aggressive display, and some of the working girls whooped their appreciation as well. Placing one hand on Slocum's shoulder, she used the other to pluck the hat from his head and place it on top of hers. Kelly then wrapped her arms around his neck and pressed her lips hard against Slocum's mouth.

For the next few seconds, Slocum couldn't hear much apart from his own breathing and the wailing crowd. He waited to hear a gruff voice calling him out or even feel a callused hand pull him up from his chair, but none of those things were forthcoming. When the kiss ended, Kelly leaned back just enough for him to see her face.

"Just sit there and look happy," she whispered.

"No problem there."

"Follow my lead and do what everyone else is doing. People here are grinning and misbehaving. If we do the same, we'll blend in like just two more weeds in a garden."

She leaned back a bit and reached between Slocum's legs to rub the bulge that was growing there. He tensed at her touch out of surprise more than anything else, and when he glanced down, he was treated to a pleasant sight. She'd pulled her shirt open just enough to expose the tops of her pert breasts and the undershirt that was plastered to her skin by the sweat that had soaked through the thin material. Although her appearance and behavior would have created a spectacle anywhere else, Slocum only had to look around to notice that several other men seated nearby were getting a whole lot more from women dressed in a whole lot less.

"There's only two of them," Kelly whispered.

"Is . . . is Scott with them?" Slocum asked while doing his best to maintain his focus.

Kelly massaged him as if she was barely aware of what her hand was doing. Even though her motions were just a facade, they were well practiced and having one hell of an effect on him. "Which one is Scott?"

"Shorter fellow. Bald head . . ."

As Slocum trailed off, she looked down at him and grinned. Her hand cupped him and she stroked every inch of his hard shaft through his pants. "Having some trouble concentrating?" she asked.

"Maybe you should ease up on me until my head clears."

"You really want that?"

"No," Slocum replied. "But I also don't want to leave

myself open to being shot at when we could be getting the hell out of the line of fire."

"Don't worry about it," she told him. "They're already gone."

Lifting her up so he could twist around in his seat, Slocum glanced toward the back hallway. It was difficult to see anyone in particular through all the general mayhem within that saloon, but there was no sign of anyone forcing their way inside. As far as he could tell, Scott was gone.

"Maybe we should just stay here," she said while settling into Slocum's lap. "I'm getting pretty comfortable."

"We probably shouldn't push our luck. If those men come in here and decide to start shooting—"

"If anyone comes into this place with guns blazing," Kelly cut in, "then they're too stupid to survive."

"Yeah. I suppose you're right."

"Why are you in such a hurry to leave?" she asked while stroking him until his penis was rigid as iron.

"We can't just sit here," Slocum said. "Besides, don't you want to go check on your friend?"

Kelly's playful smirk quickly faded. Placing her hands upon his shoulders, she said, "Brackett's dead. If the bullet or the fall didn't do the job, then one of those men must have finished him off."

"We should make certain of that. If he's just wounded and managed to drag himself away somewhere, he'll be needing help."

For a few moments, Kelly was quiet and very still. The only part of her that moved was her hand as it eased out from between his legs. "You're right," she said. "Let's go."

"Did you scout a good way for us to slip out of here?" Slocum asked.

She looked at him and showed him a warier version of

her previous smile. "I thought the front door would do just fine."

Slocum's entire body was tense when he stood up from that chair. Of course, some parts of him were tenser than others for very different reasons. When no angry voices or gunshots came his way, most of his muscles relaxed.

"You takin' that one for a while?"

Slocum almost ignored the question until he realized it was meant for him. One of the men seated at a nearby table leaned back and glared at him through drunken eyes. A woman straddled his lap with her skirts hiked up and the top portion of her dress opened to reveal a set of plump breasts. She faced away from the man, grinding in his lap and looking toward the bar.

"I had my eye on that one there," the man in the chair said while nodding toward Kelly.

She pulled her shirt closed after climbing off Slocum and started walking toward the front door. "I bet you have."

Watching her leave, the seated man grunted, "Save some for me, mister."

Since he couldn't decide whether he should say something back to the other man or punch him in the face, Slocum opted to just turn his back on him and walk away. Kelly was already outside. She'd stopped after stepping through the front door, but only long enough to get her bearings. Now that she had them, she turned sharply on the balls of her feet and started walking.

She took a roundabout course to retrace their steps and wound up in the vicinity of Mickey's. When they got closer to the building where Brackett had been posted, Kelly stopped and gazed up at the roof.

"There's no way he could've made it," she said.

"It is pretty high up."

"He would've picked the highest spot he could find."

"Makes sense," Slocum replied.

Turning her eyes toward Mickey's, she added, "Connell's gone, too."

"He's that big fellow who jumped me back in Pico Alto?"

"That's him. He went inside that place to get a look. Never came out."

"He could have gotten away," Slocum offered.

After a moment or two, she shrugged. "I suppose."

"Do you have a place where you were staying here in town?"

"Of course I do. I'm not about to sleep with my horse," she said with a laugh. "Or any of these filthy killers."

"So . . . maybe we should go there. Just in case one of your friends turns up."

Kelly was still wearing Slocum's hat and moved it forward so it was covering more of her face. Turning her head and walking behind a small group of drunks to avoid being seen clearly from Mickey's, she shifted into a more purposeful stride. "They're not my friends," she told him.

Falling into step beside her, Slocum looked at Mickey's just long enough to also become suspicious of the men leaving it. Scott wasn't among them, but the faces he saw were all sharp eyes and stern lines. Before any of those eyes could find him, he shifted his shoulders forward and turned away from them. "All right then," he replied. "Partners."

"Partners have your best interests at heart."

"Usually," Slocum said. "But not always."

"Those two who were working with me didn't even have each other's interests in mind. They were soulless animals."

"Then why were you working with them?"

Without missing a beat, Kelly said, "Because Connell

was strong as an ox and could take a punch. Brackett was a hell of a good shot. Both of them were greedy enough to stay on task until the job was done. After that, they were going to kill me."

"You're sure about that?"

"Pretty much."

"No honor among thieves, huh?" Slocum scoffed.

"Never has been. Never will be."

"You seemed worried about him before. It didn't exactly set right with you when he was gunned down off that roof."

Kelly walked past the next building and turned. Although there was a large space between it and its neighbor, there wasn't a proper street there. Even so, ruts in the ground and multiple sets of overlapping tracks made it clear that it got more traffic than just another alleyway. "He was great at his job. You saw that much for yourself. I didn't trust him, but it wasn't easy to see him killed. You must've seen plenty of men get killed," she added while turning to look back at him. "It never gets easy, right?"

She was right. Slocum had indeed seen plenty of men get killed. As far as it never getting easier, he had to disagree. Watching men die did get easier. It was a shame to admit as much, but it was true.

"Brackett did a good job in covering us," she said. "I knew he would."

"Spoken like someone accustomed to wrapping men around her little finger," Slocum grumbled.

"No. Spoken like someone in charge of gathering up the money and splitting it up. Once that was done . . ." She made the shape of a gun with her fingers, pointed it to her head, and pulled the imaginary trigger. "That's why Brackett was such a great partner," Kelly said almost wistfully. "We both knew exactly where we stood with each other."

"And what would have happened once the money was split up?"

She slowed her pace to a leisurely walk and glanced upward. Continuing to move her head until she was looking over at Slocum, she said, "Things would have gotten interesting. That's all I know for certain, which is the way I like it. Once you figure every angle with absolute certainty, life becomes tedious. I can't abide tedious."

"What about that fat man at the saloon back there?" Slocum asked. "Was he another partner?"

"No," she said with a laugh. "He was just another man who wanted to believe he could get his hands on me after a small amount of work. Those ain't exactly in short supply."

Even though nobody was charging at them right then and there, Slocum was still uncomfortable walking the streets. The rough stretch of road widened into a spot where buildings lined both sides. Unlike a normal street, this one felt more like an accident. Some storefronts faced the walkway and others were turned the opposite direction. Some of the entrances to the saloons or gambling dens were obviously back doors that had been hastily fitted with sturdier stairs or pieced-together porches. For any other town, the sight would have been a strange one. For Saint's Row, it felt like a pleasant change of pace.

"So I take it that Scott fellow isn't your partner?" Kelly asked.

"I guess not. Right now, I'm not certain just who the hell he is."

"I've been in that spot once or twice," she said as if confiding in a friend. "Since then, I've found it's better to be the one doing the double-cross instead of the one being crossed."

"A thief who 'fesses up to her own nature," Slocum mused. "That's actually kind of . . . refreshing."

She shrugged. "I know who I am. You know who I am. We both know who you are. We're both getting shot at by the same people. Might as well talk straight with each other while we can."

"At least, until things get interesting, right?" Slocum asked.

"Exactly."

"So where are we headed?" When he saw the sideways glance Kelly gave him, Slocum added, "Since we're both being straight with each other and all."

"It's a safe place where we can wait for those gunmen to lose interest. Or at least wait for them to cool their heels a bit."

She led him to a shabby little cathouse in the middle of town. Once he was inside the place, Slocum guessed it could have been the oldest cathouse in town. Every wall of the structure, inside and out, looked as if it had been baked in the California sun for far too long. Even the doors were too warped to close properly, leaving a small gap at the top and bottom of their frame once they were closed. On their way to one of the private rooms, Slocum passed everything he might expect to find in a cathouse. There was a bar, a few burly fellows carrying clubs or shotguns to guard the girls, and there were the girls themselves. It wasn't a bad selection for such a filthy little town. In fact, the generally good condition of the girls helped form Slocum's opinion that the cathouse was more established than most. Then again, there was always the possibility that a town of outlaws simply preferred to bring in whores that were of a higher quality than the whiskey.

Kelly's room was a small one at the end of the hall on the second floor. It was just large enough to contain a small bed on a broken frame, a dresser with two drawers, and a padded stool. Owing to the condition of the door, it barely felt like they were inside a room at all after it was closed.

"It's not much," she said as she went to a narrow window to get a look outside, "but it's free of charge."

"How'd you manage that?" Slocum asked. "Next to nothing in a cathouse is free."

"For a man, that's true. For someone like me, however, it's a different story. And before you get any notions about me cavorting with any of these women, I'll have you know that any working girl can appreciate someone who takes the initiative and fends for herself."

"Is that what you call stealing horses or anything else that's not nailed down? Taking the initiative?"

"Yep," she replied. As she reached for the buttons on her shirt, it quickly became obvious that she wasn't trying to straighten them after hastily closing her shirt back at the other saloon. "And don't worry about either of my partners. They don't know about this room. Anytime I go into a town, I arrange for a place I can go if things get bad between me and them."

"So . . . you don't think they're dead?"

"Brackett is, for certain. Seeing as how those gunmen poured out of Mickey's without anyone shooting at their backs, I'd say Connell is as well. He headed in there right before you and that bald bastard showed up. If Connell isn't dead, he played some part in all that shooting."

"Or," Slocum offered, "he just didn't do anything to stop it."

"Either way, I don't want any part of him anymore. Connell always was something of a daisy. Funny, but the big ones often are. He wouldn't stop whining after you shot him in the foot, and you only clipped one toe."

Slocum stood with the backs of his legs touching the

edge of the bed. Even with Kelly standing by the door, she was close enough for Slocum to smell the scent of her skin as she finished unbuttoning her shirt and peeled it off. She left the undershirt in place. It was twisted around her body after so much shifting, making it seem as if it had been hastily painted onto her flat stomach and lean body. When she began tugging at her jeans to pull them down, Slocum followed suit by unbuckling his belt.

"I suppose this is how one passes time while in a cathouse," he chided.

Kelly smiled and slid out of just enough clothing to be naked from the waist down. "Just finishing what I started back at the saloon. It's only fair after me getting you so worked up."

"So," Slocum said while placing his hands on her hips. "This is where things get interesting."

"Oh, yes."

16

Once again, Kelly's hand wandered between Slocum's legs. Unlike the last time, however, her touch was warm and gentle. She found his rigid member and stroked him as if she was studying every inch. She cupped him while opening her mouth to slip her tongue past his lips. Slocum's entire body responded to her. His erection became harder. His arms wrapped around her tightly and his hands ran up and down her body. Even his breathing became faster.

She pulled off his shirt without breaking from their kiss. When Slocum reached around to cup her tight little backside, Kelly hopped up into his arms and wrapped her legs around him. For a while, they stood there entwined in each other's embrace. Their lips were pressed tightly against each other's mouths. Kelly's hips eased into just the right spot so she could feel his cock where she wanted it. She then began grinding back and forth, rubbing her pussy against his rigid pole until the lips between her legs became wet with anticipation.

Slocum could wait no longer. He set her on the bed, where Kelly immediately lay down and spread her legs open wide for him. She tugged at the bottom of her undershirt with one hand while idly rubbing her pussy with the other. Even though her undershirt remained on, it clung to her tightly enough to accentuate the slopes of her pert breasts and the bumps of her hard little nipples. Slocum stood at the edge of the bed and reached down to place his hands on the front of her body. After caressing her tight, heaving stomach, he slid them upward to massage her tits.

Pressing her hands on top of his, Kelly groaned, "Don't make me wait for it, John. Please."

Slocum was more than happy to oblige. Keeping one hand where it was, he used the other to guide his cock to the thatch of downy red hair between her thighs. Once there, he plunged into her and let out a long, satisfied breath.

"Damn, you feel good," he sighed.

Kelly smiled, closed her eyes, and arched her back. She reached out to place her fingers on Slocum's hips as he began thrusting in and out of her. Eventually, she lifted her hips so Slocum could bring her slightly up off the bed and pound into her harder. Kelly clawed at the mattress, turning her head and grunting every time his cock drove into her.

After a short while, Slocum eased out of her and set Kelly down. When she looked up at him for an explanation, he said, "Turn around."

A wide, beaming smile appeared on her face as she eagerly got onto her knees and put her back to him. Since the bed and room were so small, she was able to reach out and grab on to the edge of the dresser while her knees were perched upon the edge of the mattress. Then she arched her rump into the air and waited.

Slocum ran his hand down her back, resting it at the base of her spine, where two little dimples marked the slope of her buttocks. He moved his hands lower, feeling how her tight little ass filled them. When she dropped her chest down lower and lifted her ass just a bit more, Slocum got a real good look at the glistening lips between her thighs. First, he slid his fingers along them. Then, on a whim, he dropped to his knees and licked her pussy.

Judging by her sharp intake of breath, Kelly wasn't expecting that. She wasn't about to move, however, since that might have caused him to stop what he was doing. As his tongue flicked against her sensitive skin, her entire body started to tremble. It quaked with pleasure when he found her clit and licked it in small, quick circles.

"God," she moaned. "Oh yes! Right there. Oh, God!"

Kelly's climax was so powerful that she pulled the dresser closer to the bed. Before she had time to recover, Slocum stood up and entered her from behind. He put both hands on her hips, gripped her tightly, and started to pump in and out. Sweat ran down Kelly's bare flesh and soaked into her undershirt. Slocum slipped his hands up underneath the one piece of clothing she wore so he could fondle her tits while fucking her. Still reeling from her orgasm, she merely groaned with pleasure as he filled her with his rigid member.

Her pussy gripped him tightly and was slick with her juices. Pulling her toward him, Slocum drove his cock in as deep as it would go and held it there for a few seconds. He eased partly out of her and then pounded in again. Kelly responded with an even louder groan as she clawed at the bed like a cat. The sight of that from his vantage point was sweet indeed, and Slocum indulged himself by driving his stiff cock into her again and again until he could feel the tension inside him climb to its boiling point.

When the end drew close, Slocum pumped into her a few more times with enough force to rock the bed on its broken frame. Kelly screamed as another orgasm engulfed her, and Slocum buried himself between her legs one last time before exploding inside her. He arched his back, gripping Kelly's hips until the sensations had swept all the way through him. Even after they'd settled down somewhat, he wasn't quick to let her go.

Sometime later, Kelly lay sprawled on the bed. Her slender body took up nearly all of the mattress, and a few of her extremities dangled over the edges. Still dressed only in her sweat-soaked undershirt, she lay on her stomach after their second round of lovemaking. Slocum sat on the padded stool with his back resting against the wall. Even if he were to slip off, there wasn't much of anywhere for him to fall. He may have dozed off for a minute or two, but Slocum was fairly certain he'd kept his wits about him.

Shortly after sitting down on the stool, he'd spotted the pile of Kelly's things in a corner at the back of the room. It was just a satchel and some clothing but he figured now was as good a time as any to get a closer look. Pulling in his legs, he'd barely managed to lift himself off the stool when Kelly's tired voice drifted through the air.

"Gonna try to rob me for a change?" she asked.

"No. Just thought I'd have a look to see if you might have come into possession of something I need."

She grinned, rolled onto her side to face him, and propped her head up with one arm. "I thought I just gave you something you needed," she said while draping her other hand over one bare hip.

Slocum stood up and leaned forward. "You certainly did," he said while giving her bottom a playful smack. "What I'm looking for isn't nearly as interesting as all that."

"I can't have you rooting through my things."

"Really?"

"Yes, really," she said indignantly. "It's rude." Angling her body so she could open her legs enough for him to see what she was offering, she added, "If there's anything you're after . . . anything specific . . . just tell me."

As much as he wanted to take her one more time, Slocum said, "I'm after what you took from me back in Pico Alto."

"You mean the watch? I thought you already got that."

"No," Slocum said as he reached past her. "Not the watch."

"The money, then? As I recall, you didn't have much on you when Brackett and Connell introduced themselves."

"Right. They introduced themselves to the back of my head. I'm not talking about the money." He paused before grabbing the satchel. Looming over her like the sword of Damocles, he said, "I'm talking about what you took from my room when you went back to see what else you could pilfer."

"I didn't go into your room back in Pico Alto."

He shifted his weight so he could pin her between both of his arms. Anger rose in his voice when he said, "Don't split hairs with me, Kelly. Or Heather. Or whatever the hell your name is. Back in Pico Alto, you picked my pocket and stole my hotel key. While you kept me busy, one of your partners went back to that room and had a look around. They were real careful about putting things back the way they were, but I know they were there so don't try to deny it."

"Oh," Kelly replied as if she'd just remembered someone's name. "Now I know what you're talking about. There was some more money."

"And?"

Her eyes narrowed. "And some papers. That's all they told me they found in your room, John. I swear."

He studied her as she studied him. Every word she said to him was like a slow dance similar to the one their bodies had gone through earlier. Each of them was waiting for the other to slip up and give them some piece of information. Rather than risk giving her too much, Slocum continued the dance.

"What papers?" he asked.

She grinned. "They were in your saddlebag. You should know what they are."

"They weren't for me."

"Really?" she asked with a spark of interest that flickered like a candle behind a drawn curtain. "Whose were they?"

"You should know, shouldn't you?"

"Why?"

Suddenly growing tired of the dance, Slocum reached past her for the satchel. He'd gotten what he'd needed from her and doubted she would let any more slip. "You know goddamn well why." Once he had the satchel in hand, he backed away from the bed. He could take only about half a step back before he ran the risk of backing into the door. Holding the satchel in front of him, he asked, "Are you really going to make me sift through this? I'll tell you right now that if you act surprised with what I find, I'll be mighty cross."

For a second, it seemed she was going to position herself in an even more provocative pose on the bed. Then she decided against it. Perhaps she'd had a quick jolt of common sense. "All right," she sighed. "Go ahead and open it. See for yourself since it's so damned important."

As Slocum opened the satchel, Kelly collected some of

her clothes. By the time he'd found the folded piece of paper stuck inside a book, she was climbing into her jeans. The writing on the spine of the book marked it as a collection of poems.

"At least you didn't hide it inside a Bible," Slocum said as he tossed the book back into the satchel. "That kind of hypocrisy can get you into some pretty hot water."

"I don't know why you're so worked up about one piece of paper," she said. "It can't be worth more than the money we took from you."

"Oh, so I'll just burn it to keep you from it."

Kelly's eyes snapped back to him. Although they didn't reveal much, the subtle movement proved that she was very interested in whether or not he would follow through on his threat. If that was the case, then that paper meant something more to her than just another crumpled slip of pulp.

Holding the paper between two fingers, Slocum flipped it around so she could see the writing on its surface. "Why did you take this?"

"I already told you. I didn't take it."

"Then why did your partners take it? For that matter, why the hell would you keep it after they took it?"

"It's important."

"Why?"

"You know why," she said.

Resisting the urge to crumple the paper and grind it into dust, Slocum growled, "Enough with the sparring! However this started, it's plain to see that this situation has become something neither one of us expected. We're on the same side of the fence now. You're more than smart enough to know that much at least."

She nodded slowly. "I was thinking along those lines, but it seems you're still considering me just another thief."

"Spare me the sad woman routine," Slocum said. "It may work on others more than once, but it barely worked on me the first time."

"You're still a man, John," she said with a sly grin. "Which means you'll believe a lot when it comes from a woman. Let me see that."

Kelly held out her hand and Slocum was reluctant to put the paper in it. Eventually he did, but he was coiled like a spring in case he had to get it back again.

"I was hoping you could tell me something about what's written here. You know," she said while studying a section toward the bottom of the paper. "The part that talks about—"

"Enough," Slocum snapped. "This back-and-forth has gotten old. I know damn well you can't read that and I'm not about to give you a hint as to what you're missing."

Her face twisted into a wounded scowl. "Fine," she said while throwing the paper at him. "Just take it."

Slocum couldn't help laughing as he caught the piece of paper that fluttered in front of him. "I've got to hand it to you," he said while turning the paper so it wasn't upside down. "It takes a whole lot of gall to act offended while bickering over things that you stole with the man you stole them from."

By the way she shrugged at him, Slocum hadn't told her anything she didn't already know. "So . . . what is that anyway?"

"You don't know?" he asked. "Then why was it taken from me? And why do you still have it?"

"You're right," Kelly sighed. "This back-and-forth *has* grown old." Despite what she'd just told him, she still seemed reluctant to part with any information. Finally, she managed to overcome her natural instinct and told him,

"My partners searched your room while I kept you busy, just like you said."

"Go on."

"When he found those papers, Brackett didn't know what to make of them."

Slocum had always imagined Brackett as the one doing the searching. The notion of Connell doing it struck him as almost as likely as a bull sneaking through a china shop instead of busting straight through to the other side.

"He was going to leave them," she continued, "but they struck him as strange so he took one page so I could have a look. When I saw what was written on it . . . I thought maybe it was in some other language. I meant to throw it away at first. Then I wondered about a few things."

Seeing that she was having some difficulty confiding in him without any reciprocation, Slocum said, "You wondered why papers with gibberish on them were hidden."

"Yes!" she said, appearing to grow more comfortable right away. In fact, she even sat straight up and pulled her legs in front of her as if she were gossiping with a friend. "When Brackett told me about the compartment in that saddlebag, it wasn't anything too new. I've come across those flaps before and usually there's something real good underneath 'em. Usually deeds or money or even a will. I actually found a man's will in a compartment similar to that one. If not for them being hid away like that, those papers of yours wouldn't have struck me as much of anything. But when I heard about how they were tucked away like a treasure," she said with mounting excitement, "I thought I'd take a closer look."

Slocum nodded as he listened, thinking back to the reservations he'd had about putting the papers behind that flap in the first place. Sometimes hiding something was enough to make it look valuable, which was exactly what had happened here. In the end, it had been Captain Vicker's decision to use the fancy saddlebags he'd requisitioned for the task.

Kelly's eyes were wide open and fixed on Slocum. When she spoke, it was in a hurried string of words that had probably been bottled up inside her for quite some time. "I don't know many other languages, but what I saw on that paper didn't look like it could mean much of anything to anyone. There was just something strange about it, you know?"

If she was still trying to get him to part with something, she was mighty good at her job. Even with his guard up, Slocum had a hell of a time fighting the urge to join into the conversational spirit. Instead, he just kept nodding and watching her with stern eyes.

"I even took them to someone who might know a thing or two about what language or whatever it might have been," she said.

Slocum could feel the shift in his features, but didn't care. At this point, if she didn't know he was hanging on what she was saying, Kelly was blind as a bat. They were both too deep into this affair to pretend they weren't. "Really?" he asked. "Who did you take it to?"

She wagged a finger at him as if she were gently scolding a child. "You know I can't tell you that. A girl's got to have her secrets."

"You have something to say—otherwise you wouldn't have even started down this road."

"I don't have much experience in this area, but I do know a few men who dabble in some interesting fields. One of them is stationed not too far from here and he had a few things to say."

Stationed usually meant military. Slocum had to

wonder if she'd let that slip on purpose or not, but he decided it didn't matter at this point.

"He said it could be some sort of code," she went on to say. Once again, her eyes narrowed. If they were sitting across from each other at a card game, Slocum would have pegged that as one of her tells.

"I suppose he cracked it for you?" he asked without giving anything away that she might be able to add to her theory.

Kelly's hopeful expression dropped a bit as she said, "No, but I know it's important because less than an hour after I left him, men were trying to kill me."

"Just men?"

"And one woman." Her brow furrowed as she leaned in closer. Dropping her voice to a whisper, Kelly asked, "Did you already know about that?"

"That depends. What did this woman look like?"

"A bit shorter than me. Light brown hair."

"Crazy eyes," Slocum added. "Liked to work with knives?"

Kelly smiled. "You've met her, too."

"We've been introduced. Can't say as it was as good as the first few times I met up with you."

"Few things are as good as that," she boasted. "Let me guess. She tried to kill you."

Slocum feigned astonishment. "What? You don't think she would want to seduce me first?"

Shaking her head, Kelly replied, "Anyone with eyes like that isn't exactly interested in that sort of thing. At least, not before she's interested in sticking you with one of her blades."

"Sounds to me like you had a similar experience."

"It wasn't long after I left that friend of mine when someone came after me asking about the paper. Actually, they wanted all of the papers. At first, I regretted not getting all of them while I had the chance. That way, I could have bartered a good price for handing them over. Those men came at me pretty hard, but I don't think they were expecting to have such a fight on their hands. What with me being a mere slip of a woman and all," she said in an affected tone of voice.

"So you had a chance to talk to them."

"Yes, but not for very long. They followed me back to the stable when I went to collect my horse, asked for the papers, and when I asked too many questions in return, they started getting rough. Since I only had the one paper, I figured I didn't have much to bargain with so I tore out of there as best I could."

"Since you're alive," Slocum said, "your best must have been good enough."

"They were taking it easy on me." Judging by the way she spat out those words, it was obvious she resented every last one of them. "But that won't happen again."

"How many of them were there?"

"Four. The one who did all the talking was a dandy of a fellow with long hair. Handsome man," she said as if she were about to lick her lips. "The woman rode beside him. The other two were just gunhands. They hung back, watching me like dogs who didn't know much of anything else. I barely got out of that stable alive. Took me a while to catch up with Brackett and Connell. Longer than usual. I suspect one or both of them sold me out to that dandy and his knife woman."

"My money would be on Connell," Slocum offered. "Seeing as how he went into Mickey's just before hell cracked open and spilled all over us."

"Could have been Brackett just as well," she said. "They might have killed him to avoid paying him."

"Did you forget that he killed one or two of them so we could get off that street?"

The pang of sorrow that flickered across her face told Slocum that she hadn't forgotten. Kelly stuffed that slip of emotion down deep with the others that were surely kept out of sight from the rest of the world and looked up at him. "You're right," she said. "It was probably Connell. They're not the only ones I've worked with, though. For all I know, the man I went to for the translation may have sold me out. In this world, it always boils down to looking out for your own hide. Everyone else is a liability."

"And you were right about one thing."

"Just one?" she said though half a giggle.

Slocum held up the paper. "This is important and there are plenty more men that are willing to kill for it. Perhaps we should count ourselves lucky that we've only got four to deal with right now."

"I don't know. Those four seemed awfully damn capable."

"Then why don't we get moving before they know we're gone?"

Studying him carefully, Kelly asked, "Did you say *we*?"

17

"So, let me get this straight," Kelly said as she rode beside Slocum early the following morning. "You want me to come along with you to return this page to . . . where again?"

Although they'd spent a good portion of their remaining time in Kelly's borrowed room talking about the day ahead of them, an even larger portion was spent with Kelly showing Slocum a few of her other talents. Afterward, the two of them rode down one of the wider alleys that passed for side streets in Saint's Row. It was just past dawn, and even though they hadn't gotten much sleep, both were more than ready to put the mangy little town behind them.

"It's going," Slocum replied, "to where it needs to go. You'll find out once we get there."

"Ah. I suppose you don't want to tell me in the event that I might try to stab you in the back?"

"Something like that. There's also the chance that you may get captured and forced to talk. This way—"

"This way," she interrupted, "I can be tortured without having anything to tell my captors to make it stop."

Slocum shrugged. "I'm sure you'd think of something to say. Isn't that your strong suit?"

"One of them."

"And how am I supposed to believe you'll hold up your end of the bargain?" she asked.

"I told you there's a payment coming once this page is delivered," he said. "I promised you'd get some of that payment as long as you earn it."

"Isn't handing over that page enough to earn something?"

"Sure," Slocum replied. "How about you hand over some of that money you stole from me so I can give a portion back as a reward?" After taking a moment to let that sink in, he added, "Your payment for that paper is me forgetting about the money you took before. If you want any more, you'll have to earn it." Seeing the salacious look that had crept onto her face, he hastened to say, "Earn it by making sure our delivery gets to where it needs to go, not by curling my toes again."

"There's still a few ways for me to curl those toes that you haven't tried yet."

"I'm sure there are." No matter how badly the rest of his body wanted to take her up on her offer, the part connected to his brain said, "The fact still remains that I don't have much to pay you until I see this job through."

"I could always take the paper back."

"You could have done that last night."

"If you weren't keeping me so busy."

"And if I'm supposed to believe you were too busy to steal from me, then you must think I'm pretty darn stupid."

Kelly shrugged. "You're a man. But . . . I suppose . . . not a stupid man." She shifted in her saddle to look behind her. Saint's Row was still visible, but it seemed more like a dirty smudge on a dusty canvas.

"Don't fret so much," Slocum said. "There's always a chance that those gunmen from the other day never did catch up to us and they're still searching Saint's Row. If we deliver this paper, then you'll get a reward for doing next to nothing."

"Nothing's ever that easy."

"You should be more optimistic."

"I might try to take a brighter outlook," she said. "But—"

The shot came from a long distance. First, Slocum heard the hiss of lead cutting through the air and then he heard the crack of a rifle shot. When he heard the slap of a bullet punching into flesh, he tensed to feel the pain of being picked off his horse. He wasn't comforted in the slightest when he didn't feel anything. He'd seen plenty of men get shot without expecting it and their faces reflected no pain whatsoever. They simply blinked and found themselves dead.

A second later, he tried to get a look at Kelly in case she was the one who'd been hit. That little attempt at movement sent Slocum reeling in his saddle. Before he could regain his balance, he was on his way to the ground. Another gunshot followed the first, coming at Slocum and Kelly as if through a vat of tar. It felt like it took an eternity for him to finally hit the solidly packed dirt, and when he did, Slocum wasn't happy about it.

His hip impacted first, followed by one arm slapping against the ground in an attempt to break his fall. Pain shot through his body, and his joints cried out in agony. Even so, it could have been a whole lot worse. When he sucked in his next breath, time snapped right back to its normal flow.

"Kelly!" he shouted.

He started to look for her, but was distracted by movement from something a whole lot bigger. His horse reared up, churning its front hooves in the air while letting out a shuddering groan. As soon as he saw the horse stagger half a step sideways, Slocum rolled away. He was barely able to clear some space before the animal dropped onto its side with a pained whinny. A bloody wound in its side told Slocum where that first round had landed.

Another sound made it through the jangling in Slocum's ears. It came like distant thunder, rumbling through the ground and growing louder with every passing moment.

"Kelly! Find some cover!"

"Really?" she hissed from somewhere nearby. When Slocum turned toward her voice, he found her crouched behind a rock. "You think I should find cover, huh?" she asked. "You really are a quick thinker, John."

"Where's your horse?" he asked.

"I hopped off when they brought yours down. Figured I'd make a smaller target that way. How about you join me over here?" she said. "That idea you had about finding cover was a good one."

Between being thrown off his balance in such a sudden manner and being dumped onto the ground in a heap, Slocum's head was spinning like a top. His senses were coming back to him but only in a slow trickle. Even as another rifle shot cracked through the air, he needed a moment to figure out which way he had to move in order to crawl toward Kelly's rock. Once his limbs were beneath him and his head was pointed in the right direction, he scampered on all fours quickly enough to leave a trail of dust behind him.

His body went through the necessary motions without much direction. Those instincts took him from the spot where he'd landed and around the rock to press his shoulders against it with his legs tucked in close to his body. "What the hell happened?" he asked.

"You mean you don't recall your horse being shot?"

"I mean what happened since then?"

"It's only been a few seconds." Reaching out to place a hand on his cheek, she looked into his eyes and asked, "Are you all right?"

"I'm a bit rattled from the fall, but fine otherwise. Did they take a shot at you?"

"Yes, but they missed."

"How many of them are there?"

"Don't know yet," she said. "I haven't found an opportunity to take a good look." Just then, another shot cracked through the air. This one was fired from somewhere much closer than the rest, and it hissed within inches of the rock to thump into the dirt behind them. "And," Kelly said while ducking down a bit lower, "it looks like I'll have to wait a little longer."

18

"Neither of you is going anywhere!" someone shouted from no more than sixty yards away. "And nobody's coming to help you. Might as well hand over what we want so we can all be on our way."

"What the hell *do* you want?" Slocum shouted.

One shot was fired, followed by a whole lot more. Most of them sparked against the rock Slocum and Kelly were using for cover, and the rest dug holes into the ground on either side of them. For a while, it seemed the hailstorm of lead would never stop. The roar of the shots and the deadly barrage of bullets kept coming until Slocum found himself pressed tightly against the rock, hanging on to his Remington until his knuckles turned white.

"Jesus!" he snarled beneath the onslaught.

When the attack finally let up, he looked over at Kelly, who was drawn into a tight ball with her knees pulled against her chest, her head down, and both hands clasped on top of it. She looked up hesitantly and whispered, "Are we still alive?"

"For now," Slocum replied.

"That," the man in the distance shouted, "is what happens to people who think I'm an idiot. You know damn well what I'm after!"

"All right. Maybe I do. Why don't you come over here and get it?"

There was silence for a few seconds before a reply was given. "Fine," said the man. "Toss out the documents."

When Slocum pulled the folded piece of paper from his pocket, Kelly looked at him in disbelief. "You're going to give it to them?" she asked.

"Just be ready," he whispered. Then Slocum extended his arm to wave the paper above the rock like a flag. With the snap of his wrist, he tossed the coded document away from the rock. It landed with a slight rustle against some dirt and fallen leaves. For the next few moments, those were the only sounds to be heard.

"Keep your eyes open," Slocum said. He looked down at her hands and scowled when he found them to be empty. "Aren't you heeled?"

"The only gun I keep on me is something that can be tucked away. Anything bigger than that is with my horse, and I sent her away from here. She won't go far, but—"

Slocum let out a sigh. "There's a rifle in the boot of my saddle." He took a quick look around the rock to check which side his horse had fallen on before giving up the ghost. Fortunately, the boot was on the side facing up, and the Spencer rifle had slid partly out of its leather sheath. Unfortunately, the horse was far enough away that anyone wishing to get to it would need to break from cover to do so. Before pulling himself back behind the rock, Slocum saw a pair of men coming forward. One rode on a horse and the other kept to the side of the wooded trail, where he could easily disappear from view.

"There's two men coming," Slocum said. "Two that I can see anyway."

Kelly stayed low and leaned out to glance around the side of the rock. Quickly pulling herself back, she said, "One of them was with the dandy who came to me about that paper. Come to think of it, it may be him that's been shouting at us in between all this shooting."

"And you said there were only four of them before?"

"Yes, but that doesn't mean I saw all there was. He could have even hired on some more since I saw him last."

Slocum knew she was right on both counts, but all he had to work with was what was in front of him at the moment. For now, the only ones he could see were the two walking forward. If there were any more, they would show themselves soon enough. He didn't need to give them more time to get themselves dug in.

"How good of a shot are you?" he asked while drawing the Remington from its holster.

"Good enough to defend myself."

"What about with a rifle?"

"Better," she said quickly. "I've done plenty of hunting and—"

"Great. I already know you can move fast, so when you go out to get that Spencer rifle from my saddle, you'll be the one to fire it."

"Wait. What?"

"Move quickly, grab the rifle, and be ready to use it. Go NOW!"

His last words, spoken with such force and urgency, drove Kelly like a whip. She did indeed move quickly, and as soon as she darted away from the rock, Slocum stood up to cover her.

The two men who'd been approaching brought up their weapons, but one of them was slightly faster than the other. Slocum targeted that one and squeezed his trigger. The Remington bucked against his palm and spat its round into the quicker man's chest. That one was knocked over as if he'd been kicked by a mule, firing a round from his own pistol as he went. The man beside him carried a shotgun and started to raise his weapon to fire.

Kelly had reached Slocum's fallen horse by now and was pulling the Spencer the rest of the way from the saddle's boot. She looked up as Slocum's gunshot was still ringing through the air, saw the shotgun in the other man's hands, and moved away from the horse. Slocum and the man pulled their triggers at the same time, filling the air with thunder.

Slocum had aimed as if he were pointing his finger at his target, relying on instinct for the sake of speed. He fired at the shotgunner, throwing off the other man's aim. Buckshot ripped through the air, spreading in a deadly wave of lead that tore chunks from the dead horse's carcass. The second barrel was fired as well, but too hastily. Dirt and sparks flew as the weapon's lethal payload scratched against Slocum's rock and ripped into the ground directly in front of it.

As Kelly hurried back to him, Slocum poked his head around the side of the rock, took aim, and started firing in quick succession. At first, he didn't even see a target. His eye then caught sight of some branches among some nearby trees that had been brushed by the shotgunner who'd passed by them. The Remington barked again and again, sending its remaining rounds into the trees where the shotgunner had sought refuge. When the pistol ran dry, Slocum pulled himself back behind the rock and immediately started to reload.

Kelly was behind the rock with him again, Spencer rifle in hand. "I think I saw someone circling around to get behind us," she said.

Slocum nodded as he fit the next round from his gun belt into the Remington's cylinder. "Makes sense. They aim to keep us pinned down long enough to line up a good shot."

"You're the gunhand. What's the big plan?"

"The plan," Slocum replied as he closed the cylinder, "is for us to not be sitting here when they try to close in on us."

"Great," she sighed. "It's always nice to have an expert along."

"Where's your horse?"

Nodding toward the trees on the side of the trail opposite from where the shotgunner had gone, Kelly replied, "Over there. She's used to gunfire so she'll still be nearby."

"Getting to that horse is our best chance of getting away from this spot. Give me that Spencer."

Kelly handed over the rifle and was immediately given Slocum's Remington in return.

"You're used to shooting things at closer range, right?" he asked.

"I . . . I guess."

"Then that'll do you just fine. Make a run for your horse, and if anyone tries to get in your way or stop you, just start shooting."

"Wh-what about you?" she sputtered as more shots began to explode from the nearby trees.

"I'll be right behind you. Once you get to your horse, saddle up and wait for me until the count of ten."

"Only ten?"

"If I'm with you by then," Slocum told her, "I won't be coming. Now go."

Kelly muttered nervously under her breath. When it seemed she wasn't going to be able to dredge up the nerve to follow through on the orders he'd given her, another volley of gunfire was sent toward the rock. Slocum responded by firing back with the Spencer, which was enough to light a fire under Kelly's feet. She took a deep breath and started running before she got a chance to think of anything better.

The shotgunner who'd taken to the trees was rushing from one trunk to another, inching his way toward Slocum. Since Kelly had run in the opposite direction, Slocum allowed the shotgunner to make a little progress before taking the offensive. He sighted in on the tree where the man was hiding, fired a round that blew all the way through the trunk, and forced the shotgunner to step into the open. Once a fresh round had been levered into the Spencer's chamber, Slocum squeezed his trigger to send the other man straight to hell.

Slocum rushed out from behind the rock and snatched the paper off the ground. After safely tucking the coded document away, he headed for the trees with the rifle at his shoulder and ready to fire. Whatever he saw, he could shoot. For the first several steps, all he saw were trees and glimpses of Kelly as she led the way to their ticket out of that ambush. Shots were fired behind him, but no bullets whipped through the air close enough to garner Slocum's concern.

When he caught up with her, she was taking hold of her horse's reins and climbing into the saddle. Kelly heard him approach and turned around to point the Remington at him.

"Hold on, there," he said. "It's me."

"Good. Anyone following you?"

"Nobody right on my heels, but I've got to figure they

ain't too far behind. Let me get in the saddle and I'll pull you up."

"No," she snapped.

"What?"

A twig snapped, causing both Slocum and Kelly to look at the trees behind them. The branches there hung low to provide something of a curtain. A man stepped through carrying a gun in each hand, prompting both Slocum and Kelly to open fire. Smoke and thunder erupted from their barrels to send enough lead toward the trees to knock the approaching man flat onto his back.

Rather than wasting time celebrating their little victory, Slocum said, "We've got to go! Move!"

"This is my horse and I'm the one who takes the reins! Stop being so damned stubborn and climb up behind me."

"Aw, fer Christ's sake," Slocum grunted as he clambered up into the saddle to sit behind Kelly.

With a few sharp snaps of her reins, Kelly got the horse moving. The animal may not have been spooked by all the gunfire, but it was more than happy to put those trees behind them. As they rode, Slocum felt more uncomfortable than if he'd still been trapped behind that rock. He'd been on more horses' backs than he could count, but it was peculiar not to be in control of where he was going. His back was exposed and nearly every faculty at his command was focused on keeping his balance. Once he'd finally gotten somewhat situated, he turned to get a look over his shoulder.

After they'd ridden for another minute or two, Slocum tapped Kelly on the shoulder. "Find a place to stop," he said.

"Why? Is there anyone following us?"

"Just stop, will you?"

The trail was like most of the terrain they'd encountered that day—some rolling hills with a good amount of trees scattered as far as the eye could see. Under normal circumstances it would have been beautiful. Now there were just too many places where someone could hide. Even so, Slocum had other concerns.

Kelly picked a spot where the trail widened at a bend and steered her horse toward a meandering stream. Once there, she brought the horse to a stop and dismounted. "You really do get cross when you have to let a woman have the reins."

"Depends on who the woman is," Slocum grunted.

"I doubt that. So why did you want to stop? If it's to argue your case for being up front—"

"No. Take a look at the trail behind us."

She pulled the Remington from where it had been tucked under her belt as she stepped toward the trail. Her eyes searched the terrain like a hawk's looking for an unsuspecting mouse. Finally, she said, "I don't see anything."

"Exactly," Slocum replied. "That's not right."

"Would you prefer them to be chasing us?"

"No, but they had us in their sights. They brought down my horse with one well-placed shot."

"And we gave them enough hell to get away from there," Kelly said. "Sometimes you need to take what you can get and live to fight another day."

"Anyone who could have killed my horse that easily is a good enough shot to have hit me or at least one of us by now."

"Maybe they were aiming for you, hit the horse, and got lucky by killing the poor thing."

Slocum shook his head. "Your horse wasn't far away. Surely they could have seen it."

Moving toward her horse, Kelly reached out to pat its flank as it continued lapping water from the stream. "You make it sound like you wish they'd put my girl down along with yours."

"What I'm saying is that they let us go. It seems they got a good idea of what we're doing or where we were headed and are softening us up before we get there. That means someone was either telling them—"

"It's not me," she said quickly.

Slocum stopped her before she defended herself any further. He'd given her plenty of chances to make her play if she meant to stick a knife in his back, including leaving the document in the open for her to grab on her way out of that ambush. "I'm thinking of Scott. More than likely, whoever those others are that are trying to get this paper, he's always been in league with them. All I know for sure is that he has a bone to pick with you."

"I told you already, I haven't laid eyes on him before."

"That leaves plenty of other possibilities," Slocum told her. "He could have been the partner of someone you wronged. He could be a friend of someone who used to ride with you. It could just be that you don't recall his face. Are you telling me you'd recognize everyone you ever robbed?"

Reluctantly, Kelly shook her head.

"My point is that they had us in a tight spot and it seemed they had every angle covered, except for the ones that truly mattered."

Kelly took a deep breath. "I didn't spot anyone when I ran to my horse," she said.

"And the only shots that were taken at me didn't amount to anything but noise. For someone who was good enough to put down my horse with one shot while we were moving, that's an awfully strange coincidence."

"You think they're following us?" Kelly asked. "To find out where we're going?"

"And to see what we do once we get there. They're keeping us off balance so we'll be easier to hit once they decide to make their real move."

"This is all because of that damned paper, isn't it?"

Slocum nodded.

"Are you ever going to tell me what's on it?"

"All I can say," he replied, "is that it's important information for some important people."

"Hell," she scoffed. "I could've guessed as much. There's not going to be this much fuss over a recipe for pecan pie." Nodding to herself as she took another slow look around, she said, "There's a few things we can do. We can take them on a wild-goose chase, lead them by the nose for a while. After we get them where we want them, we can hit them just about any way we please."

"Sounds like you've had plenty of practice in that regard," Slocum said with a grin.

She returned the grin and then some. "More than you know, mister. We can get started right away and put these dogs down before we get to . . . where are we headed?"

"I'll tell you that tomorrow."

"Still don't trust me?"

"In my spot, would you trust you?"

"Guess I deserve that."

Slocum approached her, placed a finger under her chin, and lifted her face so he could look into her eyes. "Don't get bent out of shape about it," he told her. "You chose your path when you started robbing people for a living. You're a smart woman. Way too smart to be offended if I play my cards close to the vest."

"I like you, John. I'd hate to think you hold me in such low regard."

"If I thought so little of you, we wouldn't be riding together. Now let's get moving. I've got a few ideas of my own. Together, I think we can come up with something that will wrap this up nice and neat."

19

They could have made the ride to Genoa in much less time the next day, but Slocum insisted on doubling back every so often to make sure they weren't being followed. Also, he took a more roundabout route to keep any followers on their toes. He and Kelly were both convinced they were being watched, but there was no reason they should make anyone's job easier.

"So," Kelly said as they arrived in town late that morning. "Is this the place or are we still just trying to throw those gunmen off our trail?"

"This is it," Slocum replied. The moment the horse slowed enough, Slocum dropped down from the saddle and fell into step beside her.

"Afraid someone might see you riding behind a woman?" Kelly chided.

"Afraid my tailbone might get split if I take any more bumps in the road is more like it," he said while rubbing the small of his back. "I need a drink."

"The horse drinks before we do," Kelly insisted. "After all, she's the one that's been carrying a double load."

"Sounds reasonable. I'm surprised the old nag made it as far as she has."

"Don't listen to him!" she cooed while rubbing the tired horse behind the ears. "He's just a mean man in mourning for losing his own animal."

Slocum wasn't in the mood to have a conversation with Kelly and her horse, so he said, "Since you two see eye to eye, I'll let you get a stall for her. There's a stable on the corner right there. That will give me a chance to let a few men know I'm in town so we can be rid of this burden once and for all."

"Sounds just fine to me."

The two of them parted ways with Slocum walking down the street in one direction and Kelly riding in the other. The dreary storefront where Captain Vicker and Tom were waiting was just down the street a ways. Before going there, he decided to stop off at the first saloon he could find. When he got to the door of the place, Slocum felt a tap on his shoulder. He turned around and saw a pale, rounded face that had some very familiar eyes.

"You feel that?" Sarah asked.

All Slocum had to do was draw a breath to feel the blade sticking between his ribs. The tip had punctured his shirt, and if he did much in the way of movement, it would puncture a lung. "I feel it," he said.

Her eyes were just as crazy as they'd been the last time he'd seen her. "Come along with me, then," she demanded as she pulled the Remington from its holster and tucked it under her own gun belt. Now that she'd disarmed him, Sarah wrapped her arm around his as if she were being escorted to a dance. "Now start walking."

"Where are we going?" Slocum asked as he felt the knife jab against his side.

"The same way you came. Take one wrong step or do anything I don't like and your guts will spill all over this street. Understand?"

Even though he was the one with his arm looped around Sarah's, Slocum knew he wasn't in control. The way she had a hold of him, her knife was at just the right angle for it to be a constant threat without being seen. All it would take was a sharp jab from her and she'd put him down in a heartbeat.

"I understand," he replied.

"Good."

They were halfway to the stable when Slocum asked, "Is there anything I can help you with?"

"You know damn well what this is about."

"If you give me a chance to—" Slocum cut himself short when he felt the blade dig in a little deeper. It may have broken the skin by now and wouldn't take much coaxing for it to open him up even worse. He decided to keep his mouth shut for the time being.

Slocum was taken straight to the stable where Scott Jeffries waited outside the door. When Slocum got closer, the bald man grinned widely at him and held the door open so all three of them could walk inside. "Good to see you again, Slocum," Scott said.

As he stepped past him, Slocum replied, "Go to hell."

Inside the stable, Kelly was being held at gunpoint by a man with a Colt in his fist. Although she was putting on a brave front, there was definitely fear behind her eyes.

Another man leaned against the gate of the stall next to the one where Kelly's horse was being kept. In that stall was a portly man sitting, bound and gagged, upon on pile of hay. Judging by his dirty clothes and confused expression, he was just someone who'd been working in the wrong stable at the wrong time. The man leaning against the gate had long hair and wide shoulders. "My name is Duncan Shockley," he said. "One of you has something that belongs to me."

"Then why don't you just take it?" Slocum asked. "Seems like you've got enough of an advantage to do that much."

"Of course I do," Duncan said. "But you two are only carrying a part of what I need. The only reason you're alive, frankly, is because I'm quite certain you can point me toward the rest of what I need."

"And what is that exactly?" Slocum asked.

Duncan locked eyes with him and strode forward. He took a pair of brass knuckles from his pocket, slid them on, and then drove them into Slocum's midsection. Slocum doubled over, coughed up a haggard breath, and pulled himself upright again to feel Sarah's blade find its way back to his ribs.

"That's for treating me like a fool," Duncan said. "I wouldn't advise you to do that again. The pay for dealing with me in a civilized manner is much better. Just ask your friend here."

When Duncan nodded in his direction, Scott stepped forward.

"Him?" Slocum spat. "He was never a friend. He was just some asshole who tried to—"

This time, Scott was the one to punch Slocum in the gut. It was with a bare fist, but the blow was delivered into the same spot that had just been tenderized by Duncan's brass.

"That," Scott said, "is for siding with that red-haired bitch."

Slocum pulled in a slow breath. No matter how painful

it was, he wasn't about to let on that he felt the slightest effect from the pummeling he'd taken. "And you would never side with some back-stabbing woman. Oh, wait," he said while turning to look over his shoulder at Sarah. "Guess that's not exactly true, now is it?"

Seething through every pore in his body, Scott pointed at Kelly and said, "I'd rather work with the devil himself than *that* whore!"

"Hey!" Kelly snapped. "I don't even know who the hell you are!"

Scott wheeled around to face her. As he stalked forward, he seemed about ready to punch a hole through her as well as the wall behind her. "Three assholes stole everything from me and another man in West Texas. You came along and said you knew a bounty hunter that would track them down and retrieve our money for a small fee. He came back a few days later saying he found them and needed some cash to bribe a sheriff's deputy into handing them over. You said it could be an advance on the reward that was gonna be paid once your bounty hunter friend caught them again and turned them in to a sheriff in a different town."

"And you believed that?" Duncan scoffed.

If anyone else had asked that, Scott would have taken a swing at him. As it was, he bit his tongue and replied, "She was buttering me up real good, so I listened to her."

Having tasted some of that butter himself, Slocum wasn't about to cast any stones.

Turning his fiery gaze back to Kelly, Scott continued, "I handed over the advance and of course them robbers, that bounty hunter, and this bitch were all in it together. Not only did they get away with everything I had, but I had to work for months to pay back what I borrowed from my cousin for that goddamn advance!"

Everyone in the stable was quiet.

Every set of eyes was focused on Kelly.

After a few tense seconds, Kelly said, "Oh, yes. Now I remember you." Her only defense was a shrug as she explained, "We ran that routine a lot through Texas and Oklahoma. They all kind of blend together after a while."

Scott cocked his arm back. Before he could unload on her, Duncan barked, "Not yet!"

Although he was trembling with anticipation of delivering his punch, Scott obeyed and took a few steps back.

Duncan moved forward to put himself between them. "Now I can see why you were so anxious to go after this woman," he said.

"We were already going after her," Slocum pointed out. "He didn't have to side with this snake."

"Why, Mr. Slocum," Duncan said, "I take offense to that! You don't even know me well enough to call me such a thing. And as such, you can't know that I'm willing to pay handsomely to get the item I'm after. More than enough for Mr. Jeffries here to repay what he owes and have plenty left over to get the fresh start he was denied when he was wronged by this woman."

Kelly rolled her eyes. "West Texas was over a year ago," she sighed. "He can't possibly still be hurting from that."

"With a man as stupid as him," Slocum said through a grunting laugh, "it's more than likely that he was cleaned out more than a few times in a year."

Duncan shrugged. "Be that as it may, I'm willing to spread the wealth even more. I want the item that one of you two has, but as was already pointed out, I could just take it from you. What I also need is the name of the person who has the rest of the items. Surely you know what I'm talking about so don't bother asking what items. That would insult my intelligence and we all know how I feel about that."

After spitting on the ground, Slocum said, "Shove it up your—"

"Captain Vicker," Kelly said. "He's in the Army."

"You fucking bitch!" Slocum roared.

Duncan approached her and said, "Go on."

When Slocum started to say something else, he felt Sarah's blade rake against his body just hard enough to tear his shirt and draw some blood.

"We had a plan to get past you," Kelly said. "John didn't tell me much until this morning. Once we got into town, we were going to . . . well . . . it doesn't really matter anymore since you all caught up to us quicker than we were expecting."

Slocum let out a frustrated breath. Even more maddening was the smug grin etched deeply into Scott's face.

"Captain Vicker is in the Army," Kelly continued.

Duncan nodded. "I know of him."

"He's the one that's got the rest of your papers. That's what you're after, right? The rest of the papers with all the gibberish on them?"

"Yes, indeed."

"What's all that writing mean anyway?" she asked.

"Don't worry your pretty head about that," Duncan told her. "Just tell me where I can find Captain Vicker."

"We were supposed to meet up with him nearby. I can show you, but . . . how much will I get paid?"

From behind Slocum, Sarah said, "You should just be glad to be alive!"

Silencing her the way he might silence a dog, Duncan said, "If the information pans out, you'll get three thousand dollars. There may be more in your future if you prove valuable enough."

Kelly moved forward in smooth, gliding steps. Smiling at him as if she were alone with Duncan in a dimly lit bedroom, she said, "I can prove my value in many, many ways." With that, she went over to Slocum, slipped her hand into one of his pockets, and removed the folded document. "Sorry," she said to him. "It's only business."

Slocum didn't say a word.

When he got the document, Duncan unfolded it, looked it over, smiled, and then folded it back up again. "Excellent," he said while tucking the paper into his pocket. "Now . . . take me to meet with Captain Vicker."

"Of course," Kelly said as she rubbed against him like a cat in heat. "Will I be seeing John again?"

"I doubt it."

Kelly walked over to Slocum, ran her hands over the front of his body, and down to his belt. "We had some good times." It seemed as if she had more to say, but couldn't get the words out before turning away to join her new employer.

Duncan, Kelly, and Scott left Slocum with Sarah and the gunman, who had yet to say a word. Sarah walked around, slowly dragging her blade against his body, teasing him with the sharpened steel before doing any more damage. As soon as she was in front of him, Slocum brought up an arm and snapped his elbow toward her face. Sarah moved back to avoid the blow, grinning.

"I like it when they have some fight in 'em," she snarled.

The mute gunman stalked forward while raising his pistol. In one smooth motion, Slocum reached under his belt for the .32-caliber pistol that Kelly had taken from Duncan and planted on him in a series of moves that bordered on the miraculous. He squeezed his trigger twice, placing one bullet through the gunman's neck and another through his forehead.

Sarah lashed out with her blade. The knife was stopped less than an inch away from Slocum's belly when he grabbed her wrist. "This enough fight for ya?" he asked as he pulled his trigger to blow her brains out at point-blank range.

Before Sarah had a chance to fall over, the stable door opened and Scott charged inside. He was stunned to see how quickly and drastically the tables had been turned, but not too stunned to return fire. Diving into the stable, he avoided getting hit by the first round Slocum fired at him. Duncan was next to appear in the doorway and he already had his .44 in hand. He was just about to pull his trigger when Kelly hit him over the back of the head with a piece of wood she'd found outside. Instead of keeling over, Duncan dropped to a knee and rubbed the aching portion of his skull.

Scott poked his head up from behind the hay bale he'd chosen as cover and fired at the same time Slocum fired at him. Both men were too rushed to hit their targets, and while Scott's round hissed past Slocum's head, Slocum's bullet drilled through the hay bale Scott had hoped would protect him. Reflexively, Scott moved away from the insufficient barrier. He started to fire again as he moved, but Slocum was just a bit faster and his aim was good enough to burn a hole through Scott's heart with his final bullet.

Walking across the stable to collect Scott's guns, Slocum shouted, "You there, Kelly?"

"Yes," she replied before stepping into the stable.

"Where's that other one that you hit over the head?"

"He's gone. I tried to stop him, but he still had his gun. He ran down the street." Still holding the piece of lumber she'd found, she added, "I guess he's got a thicker head than yours."

"What about the paper?" he asked.

Kelly reached into her pocket and pulled out the folded document. "I lifted it from him on our way outside," she said.

Letting out an appreciative sigh, Slocum said, "You're a master of your craft."

"I know."

20

Slocum did have to answer to the town law in regard to the shooting in that stable, but after Tom Graves was informed and Captain Vicker came on the scene, the whole situation was smoothed over quickly and easily. Once he had his missing page in hand, Vicker was more than happy to let the matter rest.

"So," Slocum said as he sat in the small back room serving as Vicker's office, "what the hell is written on that paper anyway?"

"You've got your pay for the job," Vicker said. "You don't need to know any more. Sergeant Graves can see you out. We've got preparations to make. It's about bloody time we left this town."

And that was all Vicker had to say. Tom did escort him from the office, and Slocum waited until he was outside the store to broach the subject again.

"I can't tell you what's on those papers, John," Tom said in a hushed tone. "You should know that."

"I know I risked my damn life for them and I figure that should entitle me to some damn answers. Even . . . unofficial ones."

"Unofficially . . . I did hear a thing or two since the last time we spoke. Also unofficially, those documents could be orders for troop movements across the border to engage a foreign army that's got its eye on American lands."

"Mexican or Canadian army?"

"Mexican," Tom replied. "Unofficially. And the only reason I'm telling you is because I know you won't part with the information."

"Yeah, sure. So one page really was that damned important?"

"Each page is a list of names, map coordinates, schedules, armaments, troop counts, all of which form one big picture that only the generals can make sense of. Missing a chunk of that is pretty damned important. Thanks for bringing it back. We owe you plenty, and no matter how brusque the captain may be, a debt like that will be paid."

"That bonus I was paid was thanks enough," Slocum said. "If I'd known that your captain was so intent on finding this Duncan Shockley fellow, I would have tried harder to bring him in."

"You earned that bonus. Shockley turned traitor some years ago and has been selling information to foreign governments ever since. He's a ghost. Better men than you have failed to bring him in. Just knowing he's in the area vastly improves our chances of catching the bastard."

"All right, then. That just leaves her," Slocum said as he looked across the street. Kelly stood there with one of the younger soldiers dressed in a private's uniform. She was standing close to the lad, whispering things into his ear that brought a flush to the young man's cheeks.

"Vicker isn't interested in pickpockets," Tom said. "I could release her into your custody."

Slocum raised his eyebrows. "I suppose I could think of a few things to do with her."

"I thought as much. Take care of yourself," Tom said as he shook Slocum's hand. "Should I keep you in mind the next time the captain has a courier job that needs to be done?"

"Not on your life." Slocum started crossing the street, but stopped and turned back around. "On second thought, let me know if you catch up with Shockley. I still owe that dandy a few punches to the gut."

Tom gave Slocum a casual salute.

Watch for

SLOCUM AND THE CHEYENNE PRINCESS

426th novel in the exciting SLOCUM series
from Jove

Coming in August!

DON'T MISS A YEAR OF

Slocum Giant
by
Jake Logan

Slocum Giant 2004:
Slocum in the Secret
Service

Slocum Giant 2005:
Slocum and the Larcenous
Lady

Slocum Giant 2006:
Slocum and the Hanging
Horse

Slocum Giant 2007:
Slocum and the Celestial
Bones

Slocum Giant 2008:
Slocum and the Town
Killers

Slocum Giant 2009:
Slocum's Great
Race

Slocum Giant 2010:
Slocum Along
Rotten Row

Slocum Giant 2013:
Slocum and the Silver
City Harlot

penguin.com/actionwesterns

M457AS0812

GIANT-SIZED ADVENTURE FROM AVENGING ANGEL LONGARM.

BY TABOR EVANS

2006 Giant Edition:

LONGARM AND THE
OUTLAW EMPRESS

2007 Giant Edition:

LONGARM AND
THE GOLDEN EAGLE
SHOOT-OUT

2008 Giant Edition:

LONGARM AND THE
VALLEY OF SKULLS

2009 Giant Edition:

LONGARM AND THE
LONE STAR TRACKDOWN

2010 Giant Edition:

LONGARM AND THE
RAILROAD WAR

2013 Giant Edition:

LONGARM AND
THE AMBUSH AT HOLY
DEFIANCE

penguin.com/actionwesterns

M456AS0812

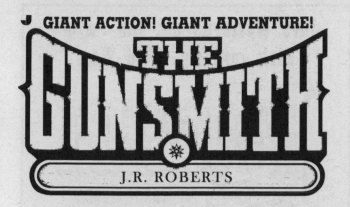

GIANT ACTION! GIANT ADVENTURE!

THE GUNSMITH

J.R. ROBERTS

Little Sureshot and
the Wild West Show
(Gunsmith Giant #9)

Dead Weight
(Gunsmith Giant #10)

Red Mountain
(Gunsmith Giant #11)

The Knights of Misery
(Gunsmith Giant #12)

The Marshal from Paris
(Gunsmith Giant #13)

Lincoln's Revenge
(Gunsmith Giant #14)

Andersonville Vengeance
(Gunsmith Giant #15)

The Further Adventures
of James Butler Hickok
(Gunsmith Giant #16)

penguin.com/actionwesterns

M455AS0812

8168

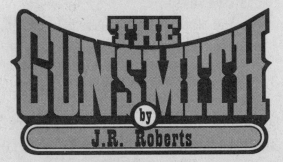